FAIRIES, ELVES AND SPRITES

Myths and Legends

More classic literature available
from Macmillan Collector's Library

Mermaids, Sirens and Selkies

Witches, Wizards and Sorcerers

Dragons, Wyverns and Serpents

Greek Myths: Gods and Goddesses

Greek Myths: Heroes and Heroines

The Odyssey by Homer

The Iliad by Homer

The Aeneid by Virgil

FAIRIES, ELVES AND SPRITES

Myths and Legends

Edited and introduced by
JEAN MENZIES

MACMILLAN COLLECTOR'S LIBRARY

This collection first published 2025 by Macmillan Collector's Library
an imprint of Pan Macmillan
The Smithson, 6 Briset Street, London EC1M 5NR
EU representative: Macmillan Publishers Ireland Ltd,
1st Floor, The Liffey Trust Centre, 117-126 Sheriff Street Upper,
Dublin 1, D01 YC43
Associated companies throughout the world
www.panmacmillan.com

ISBN 978-1-0350-3155-9

Introductions copyright © Jean Menzies 2025
Selection and arrangement copyright © Macmillan Publishers
International Ltd. 2025

All rights reserved. No part of this publication may be reproduced,
stored in a retrieval system, or transmitted, in any form, or by any means
(electronic, mechanical, photocopying, recording or otherwise)
without the prior written permission of the publisher.

1 3 5 7 9 8 6 4 2

A CIP catalogue record for this book is available from the British Library.

Endpaper pattern by Andrew Davidson
Typeset in Plantin by Jouve (UK), Milton Keynes
Printed and bound in China by Imago

This book is sold subject to the condition that it shall not, by way of
trade or otherwise, be lent, hired out, or otherwise circulated without
the publisher's prior consent in any form of binding or cover other than
that in which it is published and without a similar condition including this
condition being imposed on the subsequent purchaser.

Visit **www.panmacmillan.com** to read more
about all our books and to buy them.

Contents

Introduction vii

THE FAIRIES OF MERLIN'S CRAG 1
Elizabeth Grierson

THE TONGUE-CUT SPARROW 9
Yei Theodora Ozeki

THE NEEDLE PRINCE 25
Sunity Devee

WHIPPETY-STOURIE 38
Robert Chambers

THE HOME OF THE FAIRIES 49
Im Bang, tr. James S. Gale

PRINCESS MAYBLOSSOM 63
Madame d'Aulnoy, tr. Annie Macdonald

HILDUR, THE QUEEN OF THE ELVES 100
Jon Arnason

RHIANNON 113
tr. Lady Charlotte Guest

THE ELF MAIDEN 128
Andrew Lang

THE BANSHEE OF THE MAC CARTHYS 139
Thomas C. Croker

FORTUNÉE 165
Madame d'Aulnoy, tr. Annie Macdonald

THE LEGEND OF THE WOODEN SHOES 183
William Elliot Griffis

THE LADS WHO MET THE TROLLS
IN THE HEDALE WOOD 195
Petere Asbjørnsen

TE KANAWA'S ADVENTURE WITH A
TROOP OF FAIRIES 201
George Grey

CINDERELLA 206
Charles Perrault tr. Robet Samber

THE KILDARE POOKA 219
Patrick Kennedy

THE SUMS THAT CAME RIGHT 225
Edith Nesbit

Introduction

Jean Menzies

The fair folk, good neighbours, kindly ones, wee folk, spirits, underworldly, even gods and goddesses, call them what you will – just never call them *fairies*. This at least is the traditional advice you might receive when first uncovering the world of fairies. For to refer to them by name is a sign of disrespect, particularly according to Celtic traditions, and you definitely don't want to upset the fae. (Fingers crossed they don't read this book.)

The English term 'fairy', which I have generally opted to use throughout this collection, derives from the French word 'fée' meaning fairy, which in turn comes from the Latin 'fatūm' meaning fate in the abstract sense or 'Fāta' referring to a Fate, one of three goddesses of destiny known as the Moirai in Ancient Greek. Yet even in the seemingly simple matter of spelling you'll find your fair share of indecision – from fairy to faerie, fae to fay, and many more options in between. Although some will argue for a hierarchy of terms, many of the modern distinctions drawn between each of these names have little historicity. So, fairy it shall be.

But who, or what, exactly are these mysterious magical beings with so many different titles?

As with most of mythology and folklore, it depends on who you ask; generally speaking, however, 'fairy' is a catch-all term for such creatures as gnomes, pixies, leprechauns, sprites, pookas, boggarts, elves, peris, nymphs, banshees, mogwai, xian . . . a list which is both seemingly endless and, if I'm being perfectly frank, debatable. Aside from their temperamental nature, the real problem with fairies is that it's almost impossible to define them.

When you first read the title of *Fairies, Elves and Sprites* upon picking up this book, what image did your mind conjure? The miniature Tinker Bell of J. M. Barrie's *Peter Pan* stories? The mature fairy godmother of fairy tales, from 'Cinderella' to the *Shrek* franchise? The divine Rhiannon of the Celtic Otherworld? Or maybe the mischievous Puck of William Shakespeare's *A Midsummer Night's Dream*? All four are iconic fair folk who are distinctly different; would they recognize each other as kin were their worlds to collide? Regardless, they are equally fairies in our minds.

The reality is, fairies are a diverse and unpredictable lot. Reliably so. In fact, perhaps it is this unpredictability that is their most defining characteristic. While the tiny, winged visions from children's parties, inherited largely from the Victorians, might be kind and bubbly, the fairy folk of myth and legend are, as I've already suggested, often remarkably more sinister. Neither innately good nor bad, these magical beings have been known to use their powers for both kindness and cruelty, as you will see throughout this collection. Some are willing to help those who are modest or show them respect, while some are only interested in causing mischief or trouble, and others still just want to be left alone (oh how relatable). Some hail from an Otherworld where time passes strangely and human souls go to rest after they die. Others live in your cupboards or back gardens, in the crevices of rocks and trees, just out of sight, but never out of mind. And to meet one can be either a wonderful or terrible thing.

When it comes to their form, meanwhile, there are some who can fly, and some who can swim; some look surprisingly human, while others prefer animal form; some are tiny, some are huge; and some can appear however they choose. All of this makes compiling a collection of stories about fairies both incredibly easy and incredibly difficult. Where does one draw the line, after all?

The fairy is, in essence, a symbol of the unknown: that which we desire and that which we fear, the mysteries of life we can never truly understand, our hopes and dreams, the world beyond our own experience and following on from life itself, the natural world in all its gruesome glory. And that is what this collection contains. Stories of devious tricksters and generous guardians; tales of helpful houseguests and unpredictable visitors; fables of regal strangers and humble animals.

Within these pages you will find seventeen stories featuring fairies, elves, and other spirits (as this collection is titled), travelling around the world from Iceland to Japan, New Zealand to France, and various other places and peoples in between. Within these tales I hope you will be able to experience the diversity of the fair folk while also noting some of the qualities that seem to cross time periods and borders. These stories have been passed down in both oral and written form for centuries, between families and communities, to teach morals, to warn of dangers, and sometimes simply to entertain. So, let us continue that tradition and follow these varied and intriguing creatures into the unknown.

FAIRIES,
ELVES AND SPRITES

Myths and Legends

THE FAIRIES OF MERLIN'S CRAG

The following story was recorded by the twentieth-century author and folklorist Elizabeth Grierson. Born and raised in the Scottish Borders, we are fortunate enough as readers that through her various folk- and fairytale collections a great deal of Scottish folklore has been preserved. This specific story takes place in Lanarkshire, a historic county in the central lowlands of Scotland, in a spot called Merlin's Crag. Yes, that same Merlin who looms ever-present in the tales of King Arthur, Lancelot, Guinevere, and Morgana, and who has a surprising number of connections with Scotland. This, however, is very much beside the point as Merlin himself makes no appearance in this next story. Instead, it is a perfect example of quintessential Scottish fairy lore, containing tricky fairies and lost time. If you want a sense of Scotland's wee folk, this is the perfect place to start.

About two hundred years ago there was a poor man working as a labourer on a farm in Lanarkshire. He was what is known as an "Orra Man"; that is, he had no special work mapped out for him to do, but he was expected to undertake odd jobs of any kind that happened to turn up.

One day his master sent him out to cast peats on a piece of moorland that lay on a certain part of the farm. Now this strip of moorland ran up at one end to a curiously shaped crag, known as Merlin's Crag, because, so the country folk said, that famous Enchanter had once taken up his abode there.

The man obeyed, and, being a willing fellow, when he arrived at the moor he set to work with all his might and main. He had lifted quite a quantity of peat from near the Crag, when he was startled by the appearance of the very smallest woman that he had ever seen in his life. She was only about two feet high, and she was dressed in a green gown and red stockings, and her long yellow hair was not bound by any ribbon, but hung loosely round her shoulders.

She was such a dainty little creature that the astonished countryman stopped working, stuck his spade into the ground, and gazed at her in wonder.

His wonder increased when she held up one of her tiny fingers and addressed him in these words: "What wouldst thou think if I were to send my husband to uncover thy house? You mortals think that you can do aught that pleaseth you."

Then, stamping her tiny foot, she added in a voice of command, "Put back that turf instantly, or thou shalt rue this day."

Now the poor man had often heard of the Fairy Folk, and of the harm that they could work to unthinking mortals who offended them, so in fear and trembling he set to work to undo all his labour, and to place every divot in the exact spot from which he had taken it.

When he was finished he looked round for his strange visitor, but she had vanished completely; he could not tell how, nor where. Putting up his spade, he wended his way homewards, and going straight to his master, he told him the whole story, and suggested that in future the peats should be taken from the other end of the moor.

But the master only laughed. He was a strong,

hearty man, and had no belief in Ghosts, or Elves, or Fairies, or any other creature that he could not see; but although he laughed, he was vexed that his servant should believe in such things, so to cure him, as he thought, of his superstition, he ordered him to take a horse and cart and go back at once, and lift all the peats and bring them to dry in the farm steading.

The poor man obeyed with much reluctance; and was greatly relieved, as weeks went on, to find that, in spite of his having done so, no harm befell him.

In fact, he began to think that his master was right, and that the whole thing must have been a dream.

So matters went smoothly on. Winter passed, and spring, and summer, until autumn came round once more, and the very day arrived on which the peats had been lifted the year before.

That day, as the sun went down, the orra man left the farm to go home to his cottage, and as his master was pleased with him because he had been working very hard lately, he had given him a little can of milk as a present to carry home to his wife.

So he was feeling very happy, and as he walked along he was humming a tune to himself. His road took him by the foot of Merlin's Crag, and as he approached it he was astonished to find himself growing strangely tired. His eyelids dropped over his eyes as if he were going to sleep, and his feet grew as heavy as lead.

"I will sit down and take a rest for a few minutes," he said to himself; "the road home never seemed so long as it does to-day."

So he sat down on a tuft of grass right under the shadow of the Crag, and before he knew where he was he had fallen into a deep and heavy slumber.

When he awoke it was near midnight, and the moon had risen on the Crag. And he rubbed his eyes, when by its soft light he became aware of a large band of Fairies who were dancing round and round him, singing and laughing, pointing their tiny fingers at him, and shaking their wee fists in his face.

The bewildered man rose and tried to walk away from them, but turn in whichever direction he would the Fairies accompanied him, encircling him in a magic ring, out of which he could in no wise go.

At last they stopped, and, with shrieks of elfin laughter, led the prettiest and daintiest of their companions up to him, and cried, "Tread a measure, tread a measure, Oh, Man! Then wilt thou not be so eager to escape from our company."

Now the poor labourer was but a clumsy dancer, and he held back with a shamefaced air; but the Fairy who had been chosen to be his partner reached up and seized his hands, and lo! some strange magic seemed to enter into his veins, for in a moment he found himself waltzing and whirling, sliding and bowing, as if he had done nothing else but dance all his life.

And, strangest thing of all! he forgot about his home and his children; and he felt so happy that he had no longer the slightest desire to leave the Fairies' company.

All night long the merriment went on. The Little Folk danced and danced as if they were mad, and the farm man danced with them, until at last a shrill sound came over the moor. It was the cock from the farmyard crowing its loudest to welcome the dawn.

In an instant the revelry ceased, and the Fairies, with cries of alarm, crowded together and rushed towards the Crag, dragging the countryman along in their midst. As they reached the rock, a mysterious door, which he never remembered having seen before, opened in it of its own accord, and shut again with a crash as soon as the Fairy Host had all trooped through.

The door led into a large, dimly lighted hall full of tiny couches, and here the Little Folk sank to rest, tired out with their exertions, while the good man sat down on a piece of rock in the corner, wondering what would happen next.

But there seemed to be some kind of spell thrown over his senses, for even when the Fairies awoke and began to go about their household occupations, and to carry out certain curious practices which he had never seen before, and which, as you will hear, he was forbidden to speak of afterwards, he was content to sit and watch them, without in any way attempting to escape.

As it drew toward evening someone touched his elbow, and he turned round with a start to see the little woman with the green dress and scarlet stockings, who had remonstrated with him for lifting the turf the year before, standing by his side.

"The divots which thou took'st from the roof of my house have grown once more," she said, "and once more it is covered with grass; so thou canst go home again, for justice is satisfied—thy punishment hath lasted long enough. But first must thou take thy solemn oath never to tell to mortal ears what thou hast seen whilst thou hast dwelt among us."

The countryman promised gladly, and took the oath with all due solemnity. Then the door was opened, and he was at liberty to depart.

His can of milk was standing on the green, just where he had laid it down when he went to sleep; and it seemed to him as if it were only yesternight that the farmer had given it to him.

But when he reached his home he was speedily undeceived. For his wife looked at him as if he were a ghost, and the children whom he had left wee, toddling things were now well-grown boys and girls, who stared at him as if he had been an utter stranger.

"Where hast thou been these long, long years?" cried his wife when she had gathered her wits and seen that it was really he, and not a spirit. "And how couldst thou find it in thy heart to leave the bairns and me alone?"

And then he knew that the one day he had passed in Fairy-land had lasted seven whole years, and he realised how heavy the punishment had been which the Wee Folk had laid upon him.

THE TONGUE-CUT SPARROW

'The Tongue-Cut Sparrow' (or *Shita-kiri Suzume*) is a popular Japanese folk-tale that is, in essence, a morality tale. A morality tale is of course a story that teaches the reader/listener a lesson. While folk-tales don't have to be morality tales, or vice versa, there is a significant amount of overlap between the two genres, as demonstrated by this story. The author of the following version of this tale, Yei Theodora Ozaki, was a late nineteenth- to early twentieth-century folklorist and translator who adapted a great number of Japanese folk-tales into English. In this story we see that not only can fairies come in various shapes and sizes, but they might even appear disguised as a seemingly ordinary animal – like a sparrow. What the moral of this story is I don't intend to reveal, for that is something you shall have to learn yourself.

Long, long ago in Japan there lived an old man and his wife. The old man was a good, kind-hearted, hard-working old fellow, but his wife was a regular cross-patch, who spoilt the happiness of her home by her scolding tongue. She was always grumbling about something from morning to night. The old man had for a long time ceased to take any notice of her crossness. He was out most of the day at work in the fields, and as he had no child, for his amusement when he came home, he kept a tame sparrow. He loved the little bird just as much as if she had been his child.

When he came back at night after his hard day's work in the open air it was his only pleasure to pet the sparrow, to talk to her and to teach her little tricks, which she learned very quickly. The old man would open her cage and let her fly about the room, and they would play together. Then when supper-time came, he always saved some tit-bits from his meal with which to feed his little bird.

Now one day the old man went out to chop

wood in the forest, and the old woman stopped at home to wash clothes. The day before, she had made some starch, and now when she came to look for it, it was all gone; the bowl which she had filled full yesterday was quite empty.

While she was wondering who could have used or stolen the starch, down flew the pet sparrow, and bowing her little feathered head—a trick which she had been taught by her master—the pretty bird chirped and said:

"It is I who have taken the starch. I thought it was some food put out for me in that basin, and I ate it all. If I have made a mistake I beg you to forgive me! tweet, tweet, tweet!".

You see from this that the sparrow was a truthful bird, and the old woman ought to have been willing to forgive her at once when she asked her pardon so nicely. But not so.

The old woman had never loved the sparrow, and had often quarrelled with her husband for keeping what she called a dirty bird about the house, saying that it only made extra work for her. Now she was only too delighted to have some cause of complaint against the pet. She scolded and even cursed the poor little bird for her bad behaviour, and not content with using these harsh, unfeeling words, in a fit of rage she seized the sparrow—who all this time had spread out her wings and bowed her head before the old woman, to show how sorry she was—and fetched the scissors and cut off the poor little bird's tongue.

"I suppose you took my starch with that tongue! Now you may see what it is like to go without it!" And with these dreadful words she drove the bird away, not caring in the least what might happen to it and without the smallest pity for its suffering, so unkind was she!

The old woman, after she had driven the sparrow away, made some more rice-paste, grumbling all the time at the trouble, and after starching all her clothes, spread the things on boards to dry in the sun, instead of ironing them as they do in England.

In the evening the old man came home. As usual, on the way back he looked forward to the time when he should reach his gate and see his pet come flying and chirping to meet him, ruffling out her feathers to show her joy, and at last coming to rest on his shoulder. But to-night the old man was very disappointed, for not even the shadow of his dear sparrow was to be seen.

He quickened his steps, hastily drew off his straw sandals, and stepped on to the verandah. Still no sparrow was to be seen. He now felt sure that his wife, in one of her cross tempers, had shut the sparrow up in its cage. So he called her and said anxiously:

"Where is Suzume San (Miss Sparrow) to-day?"

The old woman pretended not to know at first, and answered:

"Your sparrow? I am sure I don't know. Now I come to think of it, I haven't seen her all the afternoon. I shouldn't wonder if the ungrateful bird had flown away and left you after all your petting!"

But at last, when the old man gave her no peace, but asked her again and again, insisting that she must know what had happened to his pet, she confessed all. She told him crossly how the sparrow had eaten the rice-paste she had specially made for starching her clothes, and how when the sparrow had confessed to what she had done, in great anger she had taken her scissors and cut out her tongue, and how finally she had driven the bird away and forbidden her to return to the house again.

Then the old woman showed her husband the sparrow's tongue, saying:

"Here is the tongue I cut off! Horrid little bird, why did it eat all my starch?"

"How could you be so cruel? Oh! how could

you be so cruel?" was all that the old man could answer. He was too kind-hearted to punish his shrew of a wife, but he was terribly distressed at what had happened to his poor little sparrow.

"What a dreadful misfortune for my poor Suzume San to lose her tongue!" he said to himself. "She won't be able to chirp any more, and surely the pain of the cutting of it out in that rough way must have made her ill! Is there nothing to be done?"

The old man shed many tears after his cross wife had gone to sleep. While he wiped away the tears with the sleeve of his cotton robe, a bright thought comforted him: he would go and look for the sparrow on the morrow. Having decided this he was able to go to sleep at last.

The next morning he rose early, as soon as ever the day broke, and snatching a hasty breakfast, started out over the hills and through the woods, stopping at every clump of bamboos to cry:

"Where, oh where does my tongue-cut sparrow stay? Where, oh where, does my tongue-cut sparrow stay?"

He never stopped to rest for his noonday meal, and it was far on in the afternoon when he found himself near a large bamboo wood. Bamboo groves are the favourite haunts of sparrows, and there sure enough at the edge of the wood he saw his own dear sparrow waiting to welcome him. He could hardly believe his eyes for joy, and ran forward quickly to greet her. She bowed her little head and went through a number of the tricks her master had taught her, to show her pleasure at seeing her old friend again, and, wonderful to relate, she could talk as of old. The old man told her how sorry he was for all that had happened, and inquired after her tongue, wondering how she could speak so well without it. Then the sparrow opened her beak and showed him that a new tongue had grown in place of the old one, and begged him not to think any more about the past, for she was quite well now. Then the old man knew that his sparrow was a fairy, and no common bird. It would be difficult to exaggerate the old man's rejoicing now. He forgot all his troubles, he forgot even how tired he was, for he had found his lost sparrow, and instead of being ill and without a tongue as he had feared and expected to find her, she was well and happy and with a new tongue, and without a sign of the ill treatment she had received from his wife. And above all she was a fairy.

The sparrow asked him to follow her, and flying before him she led him to a beautiful house in the heart of the bamboo grove. The old man was utterly astonished when he entered the house to find what a beautiful place it was. It was built of the whitest wood, the soft cream-coloured mats which took the place of carpets were the finest he had ever seen, and the cushions that the sparrow brought out for him to sit on were made of the finest silk and crape. Beautiful vases and lacquer boxes adorned the *tokonoma** of every room.

The sparrow led the old man to the place of honour, and then, taking her place at a humble distance, she thanked him with many polite bows for all the kindness he had shown her for many long years.

Then the Lady Sparrow, as we will now call her, introduced all her family to the old man. This done, her daughters, robed in dainty crape gowns, brought in on beautiful old-fashioned trays a feast of all kinds of delicious foods, till the old man began to think he must be dreaming. In the middle of the dinner some of the sparrow's daughters performed a wonderful dance, called the "*Suzume-odori*" or the "Sparrow's dance," to amuse the guest.

Never had the old man enjoyed himself so

---

* An alcove where precious objects are displayed.

much. The hours flew by too quickly in this lovely spot, with all these fairy sparrows to wait upon him and to feast him and to dance before him.

But the night came on and the darkness reminded him that he had a long way to go and must think about taking his leave and return home. He thanked his kind hostess for her splendid entertainment, and begged her for his sake to forget all she had suffered at the hands of his cross old wife. He told the Lady Sparrow that it was a great comfort and happiness to him to find her in such a beautiful home and to know that she wanted for nothing. It was his anxiety to know how she fared and what had really happened to her that had led him to seek her. Now he knew that all was well he could return home with a light heart. If ever she wanted him for anything she had only to send for him and he would come at once.

The Lady Sparrow begged him to stay and rest several days and enjoy the change, but the old man said that he must return to his old wife—who would probably be cross at his not coming home at the usual time—and to his work, and therefore, much as he wished to do so, he could not accept her kind invitation. But now that he knew where the Lady Sparrow lived he would come to see her whenever he had the time.

When the Lady Sparrow saw that she could not persuade the old man to stay longer, she gave an order to some of her servants, and they at once brought in two boxes, one large and the other small. These were placed before the old man, and the Lady Sparrow asked him to choose whichever he liked for a present, which she wished to give him.

The old man could not refuse this kind proposal, and he chose the smaller box, saying:

"I am now too old and feeble to carry the big and heavy box. As you are so kind as to say that I may take whichever I like, I will choose the small one, which will be easier for me to carry."

Then the sparrows all helped him put it on his back and went to the gate to see him off, bidding him good-bye with many bows and entreating him to come again whenever he had the time. Thus the old man and his pet sparrow separated quite happily, the sparrow showing not the least ill-will for all the unkindness she had suffered at the hands of the old wife. Indeed, she only felt sorrow for the old man who had to put up with it all his life.

When the old man reached home he found his wife even crosser than usual, for it was late on in the night and she had been waiting up for him for a long time.

"Where have you been all this time?" she asked in a big voice. "Why do you come back so late?"

The old man tried to pacify her by showing her the box of presents he had brought back with him, and then he told her of all that had happened to him, and how wonderfully he had been entertained at the sparrow's house.

"Now let us see what is in the box," said the old man, not giving her time to grumble again. "You must help me open it." And they both sat down before the box and opened it.

To their utter astonishment they found the box filled to the brim with gold and silver coins and many other precious things. The mats of their little cottage fairly glittered as they took out the things one by one and put them down and handled them over and over again. The old man was overjoyed at the sight of the riches that were now his. Beyond his brightest expectations was the sparrow's gift, which would enable him to give up work and live in ease and comfort the rest of his days.

He said: "Thanks to my good little sparrow! Thanks to my good little sparrow!" many times.

But the old woman, after the first moments of surprise and satisfaction at the sight of the gold and silver were over, could not suppress the greed of her wicked nature. She now began to reproach the old man for not having brought home the big box of presents, for in the innocence of his heart he had told her how he had refused the large box of presents which the sparrows had offered him, preferring the smaller one because it was light and easy to carry home.

"You silly old man," said she, "why did you not bring the large box? Just think what we have lost. We might have had twice as much silver and gold as this. You are certainly an old fool!" she screamed, and then went to bed as angry as she could be.

The old man now wished that he had said nothing about the big box, but it was too late; the greedy old woman, not contented with the good luck which had so unexpectedly befallen them and which she so little deserved, made up her mind, if possible, to get more.

Early the next morning she got up and made the old man describe the way to the sparrow's house. When he saw what was in her mind he tried to keep her from going, but it was useless. She would not listen to one word he said. It is strange that the old woman did not feel ashamed of going to see the sparrow after the cruel way she had treated her in cutting off her tongue in a fit of rage. But her greed to get the big box made her forget everything else. It did not even enter her thoughts that the sparrows might be angry with her—as, indeed, they were—and might punish her for what she had done.

Ever since the Lady Sparrow had returned home in the sad plight in which they had first found her, weeping and bleeding from the mouth, her whole family and relations had done little else but speak of the cruelty of the old woman. "How could she," they asked each other, "inflict such a heavy punishment for such a trifling offence as that of eating some rice-paste by mistake?" They all loved the old man who was so kind and good and patient under all his troubles, but the old woman they hated, and they determined, if ever they had the chance, to punish her as she deserved. They had not long to wait.

After walking for some hours the old woman had at last found the bamboo grove which she had made her husband carefully describe, and now she stood before it crying out:

"Where is the tongue-cut sparrow's house? Where is the tongue-cut sparrow's house?"

At last she saw the eaves of the house peeping out from amongst the bamboo foliage. She hastened to the door and knocked loudly.

When the servants told the Lady Sparrow that

her old mistress was at the door asking to see her, she was somewhat surprised at the unexpected visit, after all that had taken place, and she wondered not a little at the boldness of the old woman in venturing to come to the house. The Lady Sparrow, however, was a polite bird, and so she went out to greet the old women, remembering that she had once been her mistress.

The old woman intended, however, to waste no time in words, she went right to the point, without the least shame, and said:

"You need not trouble to entertain me as you did my old man. I have come myself to get the box which he so stupidly left behind. I shall soon take my leave if you will give me the big box—that is all I want!"

The Lady Sparrow at once consented, and told her servants to bring out the big box. The old woman eagerly seized it and hoisted it on her back, and without even stopping to thank the Lady Sparrow began to hurry homewards.

The box was so heavy that she could not walk fast, much less run, as she would have liked to do, so anxious was she to get home and see what was inside the box, but she had often to sit down and rest herself by the way.

While she was staggering along under the heavy

load, her desire to open the box became too great to be resisted. She could wait no longer, for she supposed this big box to be full of gold and silver and precious jewels like the small one her husband had received.

At last this greedy and selfish old woman put down the box by the wayside and opened it carefully, expecting to gloat her eyes on a mine of wealth. What she saw, however, so terrified her that she nearly lost her senses. As soon as she lifted the lid, a number of horrible and frightful looking demons bounced out of the box and surrounded her as if they intended to kill her. Not even in nightmares had she ever seen such horrible creatures as her much-coveted box contained. A demon with one huge eye right in the middle of its forehead came and glared at her, monsters with gaping mouths looked as if they would devour her, a huge snake coiled and hissed about her, and a big frog hopped and croaked towards her.

The old woman had never been so frightened in her life, and ran from the spot as fast as her quaking legs would carry her, glad to escape alive. When she reached home she fell to the floor and told her husband with tears all that had happened to her, and how she had been nearly killed by the demons in the box.

Then she began to blame the sparrow, but the old man stopped her at once, saying:

"Don't blame the sparrow, it is your wickedness which has at last met with its reward. I only hope this may be a lesson to you in the future!"

The old woman said nothing more, and from that day she repented of her cross, unkind ways, and by degrees became a good old woman, so that her husband hardly knew her to be the same person, and they spent their last days together happily, free from want or care, spending carefully the treasure the old man had received from his pet, the tongue-cut sparrow.

THE NEEDLE PRINCE

What I love about the next story is that it subverts one of the most pervasive fairy-tale tropes that I grew up with – the one in which a sleeping princess is in need of saving by a prince (think 'Snow White' and 'Sleeping Beauty'). Instead of waiting to be awoken from a death-like slumber by her true love's kiss, the princess in this tale is the one doing the awakening, and I am here for it. The tale as you are about to read it here was originally recorded by Sunity Devee, Maharani* of Cooch Behar, India from 1878 to 1932. During her life, Devee was a dedicated education advocate and women's rights activist who managed to compile the twentieth-century collection *Indian Fairy Tales* somewhere in her spare time. Two impressive women are therefore commemorated by this tale, it seems.

---

* Maharani means 'great queen' in Sanskrit and historically referred to the wife of the Indian Maharaja/King.

There was a Maharajah who had seven daughters. He loved them all equally well. Though they were all very pretty, the youngest was the best-looking of the seven, and she was the favourite of her mother. One day while they were all playing in the palace-gardens, they asked one another whom each loved most and preferred to live with. All the six elder ones said they would never like to leave their parents' home, where they were so happy, and they all preferred to stay with their own sisters. The youngest sister kept silent and never said a word to all this. Some of the elder sisters came to her and asked: "How is it that you do not join us in the talk?"

She answered softly: "I dare not; you might scold me, if you heard my view of the matter."

Then the six sisters cried out together: "What is it? What is your idea about it?"

"Won't you get annoyed if I spoke plainly?"

"Why should we be?"

"You might be," sweetly said the little girl.

"Don't be foolish," said the others. "Let us know what your idea is."

The youngest sister said: "We often hear mother say there is nobody like the husband to a woman, and that she can love no one more than her husband. I often wonder if I shall ever get married."

"And why not?" said the sisters, "Of course, we all shall, some day."

"Then," said the youngest sister, "I would love my husband most, and would always like to be with him."

"Oh, don't, don't!" they all cried aloud. "Both father and mother, hearing you speak like that, would turn you out of the house."

"Try and forget what you said," the sisters continued, "You cannot possibly love your husband more than you love us."

"Yes, I will," said the girl. "I will love my husband more than any one in this world."

"Very well, then, we will go and tell mother what you have said."

The little sister said: "Don't you know, dear sisters, how mother speaks of her childhood, how happy she was with her brothers and sisters? And now mother says that nothing would make her leave father and go back to the happy home she had in her childhood. My ideal of happiness is my mother's. I don't think any woman could be happier than mother is, and my ambition is to be like my mother."

The sisters coaxed her and threatened her, asking her to change her mind, but she would not. Then the girls ran into the house telling her they would go and report everything to their mother. The poor girl got frightened by their threat and ran out of the garden as it was getting dark, and escaped from the kingdom. She wandered in the jungle for days and roamed about until she felt she could not walk any more. She was exhausted with hunger and thirst. It was a hot day and the sun was just overhead. She sat down under a tree, thinking: "Had I been married, I might have been quite happy to-day."

While she was thus thinking, her eyes wandered and she thought she saw in the distance the outlines of a house. This new hope gave her strength and she ran in that direction. When she reached the spot, she found it was a big palace, with a beautiful garden in front; and the fountains and bandstand proved that it was a pleasure garden. She entered by the big gateway. What a grand building it was! White marble pillars and archways, marble verandahs and marble staircases! From courtyard to courtyard she walked about, but she saw nobody and could hear no voice, which alarmed her; and she wailed out pitifully: "Is there nobody to give me some food and water? I am dying of hunger and thirst."

She received no answer except the echo of her own voice. In fright she ran into one of the grand rooms and found it was a dressing-room with a delightful bathroom attached to it. The swimming-bath was filled with rose-water. As she felt hot and tired she could not keep herself from jumping into the bath, which cooled and refreshed her. When she came out she found in the dressing-room valuable *saris* and jewels, arranged near the mirror. She dressed herself in one of the *saris* and put on all the jewels and looked at herself admiringly in the mirror. Then she felt a longing for food. She walked round the courtyard and saw a room stored with nice fruit and delicious sweets. She entered and to her great delight she saw a small carpet spread on the floor, and golden plates and dishes laid with curry and rice. She sat down and enjoyed a good breakfast after many a day. She then felt happy and refreshed. She thought she would go and have a look at the rooms upstairs. She went up, and found the rooms furnished in a most luxurious style and for a long time she wondered to whom the palace could belong. "Why should a big palace like this be deserted? No one is found here and yet it is certain that somebody comes and goes, as I found the bath ready and the food cooked. Was there nobody living in this big house?" Then she walked from one room to another, and at last she came to a big room most gorgeously furnished. Inside these was a golden bed and, lo! on it lay a body. The young princess stood near the door, motionless. Could it be a dead body? Had some one come and killed the person and left the body here? Should she run away? Perhaps a giant might come to whom the house belonged. Such thoughts troubled her for some time. At last she boldly went near the bed, and found a most handsome young man's body lying on it, covered over with thousands of needles. Her loving little heart ached to see that sight and she wept bitterly over it.

"Who could have been so cruel?" she thought. "I will stay here and take the needles out. Dead though he be, his body must not be hurt." And she sat there and began to take the needles out of the body, one by one.

Fourteen days had passed, thousands of needles had been taken out of the body, only those in the two eyes were left; and the princess felt happy to think that she would finish taking out the needles that day, when she suddenly saw a woman's figure appearing at the door. The princess walked to the door and found it was one of her maid-servants. This servant had got frightened after the princess had escaped, lest the Maharajah should punish her for neglect of duty. So she also had left the kingdom the very day of the princess's flight, in search of her. She was old and ugly. The princess thanked her for having followed her there, and told her the whole story of the deserted palace. She took the servant by the hand and walked up to the bed and said: "Look at the number of needles I have taken out of his body. Is it not sad to think that this handsome young man will not get out of bed again? Is it not cruel to think that he is dead and gone?"

The old servant said: "Yes, it is."

Then the princess spoke again, and said: "It is getting so late, and I am rather tired to-day. Will you sit here? I shall go and have my bath and breakfast and then come back and take out those few needles from his eyes. But don't you touch the body."

The maid promised as she was bid, and the princess went, leaving her there. The maid thought: "Here is an opportunity for me to take the needles out;" and as she removed the few remaining needles, the dead man opened his eyes and hers was the first face that he saw. He leaped out of his bed and the maid was much attracted by his handsome looks. The youth said: "Did *you* take all the needles out of my body? Have you been here a fortnight?"

The maid replied in a faltering voice: "Yes, I took out all the needles, and I have been here fifteen days."

"In that case," said the young man, "you shall be my wife, for I shall have to marry you."

While they were talking thus, the young princess came back. Dressed in one of her best *saris*, her beautiful black hair hanging down, her valuable jewels heightening her beauty, she stepped like a goddess into the room. She saw the young man standing on the floor and their eyes met for the first time. Startled at the vision, the young man asked the maid: "Who is this fair maiden?"

"She is only my maid," the old hag curtly replied.

The poor young princess's heart sunk at these words, and she thought: "I, a princess, that servant's maid? I, who have been here for fifteen days, and who took all the needles out of the body?—and now my maid claims him to be hers! If I had but stayed a little longer, I would have taken those few needles out of his eyes and he would have been mine—and mine forever!"

While the princess thought thus, the young man was also thinking: "Why did I not see this beautiful face when I opened my eyes? If *she* had taken the needles out of my body how happy might I have been to-day!" And somehow he had a suspicion that such a lovely girl could not possibly be a maid-servant. After a few moments' silence, he said: "I am a prince. This house and this kingdom belong to me. I was under a spell that until a princess came and took the needles out of my body, I should never get back my kingdom or my rank. But as yet I do not hear the music, neither do I see any courtiers. I am obliged to postpone my marriage," he said, looking at the maid, "till I hear the sound of music."

From that day the maid became horribly cruel to the young princess. She took all her best *saris* from her, and all the beautiful jewels, in which she dressed herself, and she gave the princess coarse *saris* to wear and little to eat. She used to thrash her and would often threaten to kill her. The poor girl wept in silence and did not know where to turn for consolation. One evening she lay down in the garden and fell in a trance. Her tears rolled down her cheeks and bathed the lovely flowers; and little fairies came and danced on the blossoms near her face. One of the fairies said: "Oh, princess, dry those tears, you *will* be married to him!"

"How can I?" asked the princess. "How could he know that it was I who took the needles out?"

A second fairy said: "Oh yes, he will, he shall know it before long," and thus the fairies comforted and consoled the princess.

Many a month passed. The prince heard no wedding music.

One night the maid-servant threatened to kill the prince if he did not marry her forthwith. "Why should you not marry me?" she screamed out, "I have saved your life and you are so ungrateful that you have suspicions about it and wish to wait. What would you wait for?" They had many angry words about it and she lost her temper and repeated her threat. The prince quietly escaped from the palace and went out into the garden. It was a bright, moonlight night, and he saw the lovely princess lying near a fountain. Her long, waving black hair covered her body, and numbers of little fairies were tripping along on the hair; some were plucking flowers and some were arranging them on her head to make a crown. Her tears dropped on the flowers and the grass, forming dew-drops there. Some of the fairies were drying her tears and speaking to her, saying: "Fair princess, weep no more."

"Oh, kind fairies," cried out the princess, "tell me, tell me, how long should I wait? How could he get to know that it was I who took out all the needles from his body?"

"Oh, lovely princess," said one of the fairies, "why didst thou leave him? How did the maid come?"

"Listen to me, dear fairies. For fourteen days and nights I sat by his bed and removed thousands and thousands of needles from his body. Only a few needles were left, in his eyes, when my maid-servant appeared, and I asked her to sit by him just while I had my bath and breakfast, as I was tired and hungry. When I returned, after a while, I found the prince out of bed and standing in the room, and to my great distress I heard the maid tell him that she was the one who had saved his life. What could I do but keep quiet, as true enough she had taken out the last few needles and those were from his eyes, and the first person he had seen on opening his eyes was this maid-servant of mine?"

"Dear princess, do not cry," said the fairies. "The prince will soon come to know the truth, and will be wedded to you."

The prince heard all this, and his heart leaped

with joy. He walked slowly up to the princess and at his approach all the fairies fled. The crown of flowers was still on her head, and the creepers were still lying on her wavy hair and she looked like the queen of flowers in the garden. He knelt down by her, and taking her little hand in his, he kissed it, and said: "My beautiful bride, let us be wedded to-night, here, in this garden of flowers and fairies."

No sooner had he uttered these words than the sound of music was heard, horses neighed, elephants trumpeted with joy, conch-shells were blown, courtiers came galloping up to the palace, the whole place was illuminated in a moment, and once more the fair princess looked up into the loving eyes of the prince.

She answered him sweetly, "Prince, my master, how can you wed a servant? I am but a serving-maid, and you are a prince."

"Thou art my bride, my beautiful bride, and I shall wed thee here in thy flower-garment, which the fairies have prepared for thee," said he.

Then the Brahmins came and married them in the garden, where the prince had found his princess, who had saved his life.

After the ceremony was over, who should come but the old maid-servant, looking uglier than ever?

Seeing the prince seated with the princess, she screamed out to him: "I saved your life and you have married my maid-servant."

The prince, sword in hand, said: "Unless you confess the truth before all my courtiers, friends and relations, you shall be beheaded at once. I heard the truth from the fairies."

The old maid-servant then came out with the whole story, how the princess, a rich and powerful Maharaja's daughter, left her parents' home, how the maid had followed her, and on the fifteenth day discovered her in the room where the 'Needle Prince' was lying. She said that she had promised the princess not to touch the prince's body, but, she confessed, she had broken her promise and removed the needles.

The prince asked her: "Why did the princess leave her parents?"

"Because," said the maid, "the princess told her sisters that if she ever married, she would love her husband more than any one else and would like to be with him always."

The prince lifted the fair hand of the princess to his lips and, looking at her lovingly, said: "My beautiful bride, my little princess, there is no other couple in this world that could love each other more and we shall never, never part."

WHIPPETY-STOURIE

There is a power in a name – as our next story perfectly demonstrates. Imagine a fairy whose name is long and unusual, who makes cunning bargains, but whose power you can escape if you simply figure out their moniker . . . No, this is not the tale of Rumpelstiltskin, but rather Whippety-Stourie (although the two certainly have a lot in common). While the likely more recognizable 'Rumpelstiltskin' originates in Germany, the sinister 'Whippety-Stourie' hails from my own home of Scotland. Retold by various writers over the years, the following version is another recorded by the twentieth-century author and folklorist Elizabeth Grierson. In this version, a young woman from Kittlerumpit (a fictional Scottish village) who is down on her luck is offered assistance by a stranger and, too distressed to read the fine print, as it were, gets herself in even more bother than before.

I am going to tell you a story about a poor young widow woman, who lived in a house called Kittlerumpit, though whereabouts in Scotland the house of Kittlerumpit stood nobody knows.

Some folk think that it stood in the neighbourhood of the Debateable Land, which, as all the world knows, was on the Borders, where the old Border Reivers were constantly coming and going; the Scotch stealing from the English, and the English from the Scotch. Be that as it may, the widowed Mistress of Kittlerumpit was sorely to be pitied.

For she had lost her husband, and no one quite knew what had become of him. He had gone to a fair one day, and had never come back again, and although everybody believed that he was dead, no one knew how he died.

Some people said that he had been persuaded to enlist, and had been killed in the wars; others, that he had been taken away to serve as a sailor by the press-gang, and had been drowned at sea.

At any rate, his poor young wife was sorely to be pitied, for she was left with a little baby-boy to bring up, and, as times were bad, she had not much to live on.

But she loved her baby dearly, and worked all day amongst her cows, and pigs, and hens, in order to earn enough money to buy food and clothes for both herself and him.

Now, on the morning of which I am speaking, she rose very early and went out to feed her pigs, for rent-day was coming on, and she intended to take one of them, a great, big, fat creature, to the market that very day, as she thought that the price that it would fetch would go a long way towards paying her rent.

And because she thought so, her heart was light, and she hummed a little song to herself as she crossed the yard with her bucket on one arm and her baby-boy on the other.

But the song was quickly changed into a cry of despair when she reached the pig-stye, for there lay her cherished pig on its back, with its legs in the air and its eyes shut, just as if it were going to breathe its last breath.

"What shall I do? What shall I do?" cried the poor woman, sitting down on a big stone and clasping her boy to her breast, heedless of the fact that she had dropped her bucket, and that the pig's-meat was running out, and that the hens were eating it.

"First I lost my husband, and now I am going to lose my finest pig. The pig that I hoped would fetch a deal of money."

Now I must explain to you that the house of Kittlerumpit stood on a hillside, with a great fir wood behind it, and the ground sloping down steeply in front.

And as the poor young thing, after having a good cry to herself, was drying her eyes, she chanced to look down the hill, and who should she see coming up it but an Old Woman, who looked like a lady born.

She was dressed all in green, with a white apron, and she wore a black velvet hood on her head, and a steeple-crowned beaver hat over that, something like those, as I have heard tell, that the women wear in Wales. She walked very slowly, leaning on a long staff, and she gave a bit hirple now and then, as if she were lame.

As she drew near, the young widow felt it was becoming to rise and curtsey to the Gentlewoman, for such she saw her to be.

"Madam," she said, with a sob in her voice, "I bid you welcome to the house of Kittlerumpit, although you find its Mistress one of the most unfortunate women in the world."

"Hout-tout," answered the old Lady, in such a harsh voice that the young woman started, and grasped her baby tighter in her arms. "Ye have little need to say that. Ye have lost your husband, I grant ye, but there were waur losses at Shirra-Muir. And now your pig is like to die—I could, maybe, remedy that. But I must first hear how much ye wad gie me if I cured him."

"Anything that your Ladyship's Madam likes to ask," replied the widow, too much delighted at having the animal's life saved to think that she was making rather a rash promise.

"Very good," said the old Dame, and without wasting any more words she walked straight into the pig-sty.

She stood and looked at the dying creature for some minutes, rocking to and fro and muttering to herself in words which the widow could not understand; at least, she could only understand four of them, and they sounded something like this:

"Pitter-patter,
Haly water."

Then she put her hand into her pocket and drew out a tiny bottle with a liquid that looked like oil in it. She took the cork out, and dropped one of her long lady-like fingers into it; then she touched the pig on the snout and on his ears, and on the tip of his curly tail.

No sooner had she done so than up the beast jumped, and, with a grunt of contentment, ran off to its trough to look for its breakfast.

A joyful woman was the Mistress of Kittlerumpit when she saw it do this, for she felt that her rent was safe; and in her relief and gratitude she would have kissed the hem of the strange Lady's green gown, if she would have allowed it, but she would not.

"No, no," said she, and her voice sounded harsher than ever. "Let us have no fine meanderings, but let us stick to our bargain. I have done my part, and mended the pig; now ye must do yours, and give me what I like to ask—your son."

Then the poor widow gave a piteous cry, for she knew now what she had not guessed before—that the Green-clad Lady was a Fairy, and a Wicked Fairy too, else had she not asked such a terrible thing.

It was too late now, however, to pray, and

beseech, and beg for mercy; the Fairy stood her ground, hard and cruel.

"Ye promised me what I liked to ask, and I have asked your son; and your son I will have," she replied, "so it is useless making such a din about it. But one thing I may tell you, for I know well that the knowledge will not help you. By the laws of Fairy-land, I cannot take the bairn till the third day after this, and if by that time you have found out my name I cannot take him even then. But ye will not be able to find it out, of that I am certain. So I will call back for the boy in three days."

And with that she disappeared round the back of the pig-sty, and the poor mother fell down in a dead faint beside the stone.

All that day, and all the next, she did nothing but sit in her kitchen and cry, and hug her baby tighter in her arms; but on the day before that on which the Fairy said that she was coming back, she felt as if she must get a little breath of fresh air, so she went for a walk in the fir wood behind the house.

Now in this fir wood there was an old quarry hole, in the bottom of which was a bonnie spring well, the water of which was always sweet and pure. The young widow was walking near this quarry hole, when, to her astonishment, she heard the whirr of a spinning-wheel and the sound of a voice lilting a song. At first she could not think where the sound came from; then, remembering the quarry, she laid down her child at a tree root, and crept noiselessly through the bushes on her hands and knees to the edge of the hole and peeped over.

She could hardly believe her eyes! For there, far below her, at the bottom of the quarry, beside the spring well, sat the cruel Fairy, dressed in her green frock and tall felt hat, spinning away as fast as she could at a tiny spinning-wheel.

And what should she be singing but—

"Little kens our guid dame at hame,
Whippety-Stourie is my name."

The widow woman almost cried aloud for joy, for now she had learned the Fairy's secret, and her child was safe. But she dare not, in case the wicked old Dame heard her and threw some other spell over her.

So she crept softly back to the place where she had left her child; then, catching him up in her arms, she ran through the wood to her house, laughing, and singing, and tossing him in the air in such a state of delight that, if anyone had met her, they would have been in danger of thinking that she was mad.

Now this young woman had been a merry-hearted maiden, and would have been merry-hearted still, if, since her marriage, she had not had so much trouble that it had made her grow old and sober-minded before her time; and she began to think what fun it would be to tease the Fairy for a few minutes before she let her know that she had found out her name.

So next day, at the appointed time, she went out with her boy in her arms, and seated herself on the big stone where she had sat before; and when she saw the old Dame coming up the hill, she crumpled up her nice clean cap, and screwed up her face, and pretended to be in great distress and to be crying bitterly.

The Fairy took no notice of this, however, but came close up to her, and said, in her harsh, merciless voice, "Goodwife of Kittlerumpit, ye ken the reason of my coming; give me the bairn."

Then the young mother pretended to be in sorer distress than ever, and fell on her knees before the wicked old woman and begged for mercy.

"Oh, sweet Madam Mistress," she cried, "spare

me my bairn, and take, an' thou wilt, the pig instead."

"We have no need of bacon where I come from," answered the Fairy coldly; "so give me the laddie and let me begone—I have no time to waste in this wise."

"Oh, dear Lady mine," pleaded the Goodwife, "if thou wilt not have the pig, wilt thou not spare my poor bairn and take me myself?"

The Fairy stepped back a little, as if in astonishment. "Art thou mad, woman," she cried contemptuously, "that thou proposest such a thing? Who in all the world would care to take a plain-looking, red-eyed, dowdy wife like thee with them?"

Now the young Mistress of Kittlerumpit knew that she was no beauty, and the knowledge had never vexed her; but something in the Fairy's tone made her feel so angry that she could contain herself no longer.

"In troth, fair Madam, I might have had the wit to know that the like of me is not fit to tie the shoe-string of the High and Mighty Princess, WHIPPETY-STOURIE!"

If there had been a charge of gunpowder buried in the ground, and if it had suddenly exploded beneath her feet, the Wicked Fairy could not have jumped higher into the air.

And when she came down again she simply turned round and ran down the brae, shrieking with rage and disappointment, for all the world, as an old book says, "like an owl chased by witches."

THE HOME OF THE FAIRIES

The version of the story you are about to read was originally written down by the seventeenth- to early eighteenth-century author and governor of Seoul, Im Bang, and is taken from a collection entitled *Korean Folk Tales: Imps, Ghosts and Fairies*, in which the twentieth-century translator James Gale compiles a number of folk stories recorded by both Im Bang and the fifteenth-century writer Yi Ryuk. Within the historical setting of Im Bang's own century, 'The Home of the Fairies' follows a hard-up young man. On the road, he encounters a mysterious stranger and is taken to another world. Entering the land of the fairies is always an unpredictable adventure so, if you want to know how this particular young man fared, you will have to read on.

In the days of King In-jo (1623–1649) there was a student of Confucius who lived in Ka-pyong. He was still a young man and unmarried. His education had not been extensive, for he had read only a little in the way of history and literature. For some reason or other he left his home and went into Kang-won Province. Travelling on horseback, and with a servant, he reached a mountain, where he was overtaken by rain that wet him through. Mysteriously, from some unknown cause, his servant suddenly died, and the man, in fear and distress, drew the body to the side of the hill, where he left it and went on his way weeping. When he had gone but a short distance, the horse he rode fell under him and died also. Such was his plight: his servant dead, his horse dead, rain falling fast, and the road an unknown one. He did not know what to do or where to go, and reduced thus to walking, he broke down and cried. At this point there met him an old man with very wonderful eyes, and hair as white as snow. He asked the young man why he wept, and the reply was that his servant was dead, his horse was dead, that it was raining, and that he did not know the way. The patriarch, on hearing this, took pity on him, and lifting his staff, pointed, saying, "There is a house yonder, just beyond those pines, follow that stream and it will bring you to where there are people."

The young man looked as directed, and a *li* or so beyond he saw a clump of trees. He bowed, thanked the stranger, and started on his way. When he had gone a few paces he looked back, but the friend had disappeared. Greatly wondering, he went on toward the place indicated, and as he drew near he saw a grove of pines, huge trees they were, a whole forest of them. Bamboos appeared, too, in countless numbers, with a wide stream of water flowing by. Underneath the water there seemed to be a marble flooring like a great pavement, white and pure. As he went along he saw that the water was all of an even depth, such as one could cross easily. A mile or so farther on he saw a beautifully decorated house. The pillars and entrance approaches were perfect in form. He continued his way, wet as he was, carrying his thorn staff, and entered the gate and sat down to rest. It was paved, too, with marble, and smooth as polished glass. There were no chinks or creases in it, all was of one perfect surface. In the room was a marble table, and on it a copy of the Book of Changes; there was also a brazier of jade just in front. Incense was burning in it, and the fragrance filled the room. Beside these, nothing else was visible. The rain had ceased and all was quiet and clear, with no wind nor anything to disturb. The world of confusion seemed to have receded from him.

While he sat there, looking in astonishment, he suddenly heard the sound of footfalls from the rear of the building. Startled by it, he turned to see, when an old man appeared. He looked as though he might equal the turtle or the crane as to age, and was very dignified. He wore a green dress and carried a jade staff of nine sections. The appearance of the old man was such as to stun any inhabitant of the earth. He recognized him as the master of the place, and so he went forward and made a low obeisance.

The old man received him kindly, and said, "I am the master and have long waited for you." He took him by the hand and led him away. As they went along, the hills grew more and more enchanting, while the soft breezes and the light touched him with mystifying favour. Suddenly, as he looked the man was gone, so he went on by himself, and arrived soon at another palace built likewise of precious stones. It was a great hall, stretching on into the distance as far as the eye could see.

The young man had seen the Royal Palace frequently when in Seoul attending examinations, but compared with this, the Royal Palace was as a mud hut thatched with straw.

As he reached the gate a man in ceremonial robes received him and led him in. He passed two or three pavilions, and at last reached a special one and went up to the upper storey. There, reclining at a table, he saw the ancient sage whom he had met before. Again he bowed.

This young man, brought up poorly in the country, was never accustomed to seeing or dealing with the great. In fear, he did not dare to lift his eyes. The ancient master, however, again welcomed him and asked him to be seated, saying, "This is not the dusty world that you are accustomed to, but the abode of the genii. I knew you were coming, and so was waiting to receive you." He turned and called, saying, "Bring something for the guest to eat."

In a little a servant brought a richly laden table. It was such fare as was never seen on earth, and there was abundance of it. The young man, hungry as he was, ate heartily of these strange viands. Then the dishes were carried away and the old man said, "I have a daughter who has arrived at a marriageable age, and I have been trying to find a son-in-law, but as yet have not succeeded. Your coming accords with this need. Live here, then, and become my son-in-law." The young man, not knowing what to think, bowed and was silent. Then the host turned and gave an order, saying, "Call in the children."

Two boys about twelve or thirteen years of age came running in and sat down beside him. Their faces were so beautifully white they seemed like jewels. The master pointed to them and said to the guest, "These are my sons," and to the sons he said, "This young man is he whom I have chosen for my son-in-law; when should we have the wedding? Choose you a lucky day and let me know."

The two boys reckoned over the days on their fingers, and then together said, "The day after tomorrow is a lucky day."

The old man, turning to the stranger, said, "That decides as to the wedding, and now you must wait in the guest-chamber till the time arrives." He then gave a command to call So and So. In a little an official of the genii came forward, dressed in light and airy garments. His appearance and expression were very beautiful, a man, he seemed, of glad and happy mien.

The master said, "Show this young man the way to his apartments and treat him well till the time of the wedding."

The official then led the way, and the young man bowed as he left the room. When he had passed outside the gate, a red sedan chair was in waiting for him. He was asked to mount. Eight bearers bore him smoothly along. A mile or so distant they reached another palace, equally wonderful, with no speck or flaw of any kind to mar its beauty. In graceful groves of flowers and trees he descended to enter his pavilion. Beautiful garments were taken from jewelled boxes, and a perfumed bath was given him and a change made. Thus he laid aside his weather-beaten clothes and donned the vestments of the genii. The official remained as company for him till the appointed time.

When that day arrived other beautiful robes were brought, and again he bathed and changed. When he was dressed, he mounted the palanquin and rode to the Palace of the master, twenty or more officials accompanying. On arrival, a guide directed them to the special Palace Beautiful. Here he saw preparations for the wedding, and here he made his bow. This finished he moved as directed, further in. The tinkling sound of jade bells and the breath of sweet perfumes filled the air. Thus he made his entry into the inner quarters.

Many beautiful women were in waiting, all gorgeously apparelled, like the women of the gods. Among these he imagined that he would meet the master's daughter. In a little, accompanied by a host of others, she came, shining in jewels and beautiful clothing so that she lighted up the Palace. He took his stand before her, though her face was hidden from him by a fan of pearls. When he saw her at last, so beautiful was she that his eyes were dazzled. The other women, compared with her, were as the magpie to the phoenix. So bewildered was he that he dared not look up. The friend accompanying assisted him to bow and to go through the necessary forms. The ceremony was much the same as that observed among men. When it was over the young man went back to his bridegroom's chamber. There the embroidered curtains, the golden screens, the silken clothing, the jewelled floor, were such as no men of earth ever see.

On the second day his mother-in-law called him to her. Her age would be about thirty, and her face was like a freshly-blown lotus flower. Here a great feast was spread, with many guests invited. The accompaniments thereof in the way of music were sweeter than mortals ever dreamed of. When the feast was over, the women caught up their skirts, and, lifting their sleeves, danced together and sang in sweet accord. The sound of their singing caused even the clouds to stop and listen. When the day was over, and all had well dined, the feast broke up.

A young man, brought up in a country hut, had all of a sudden met the chief of the genii, and had become a sharer in his glory and the accompaniments of his life. His mind was dazed and his thoughts overcame him. Doubts were mixed with fears. He knew not what to do.

A sharer in the joys of the fairies he had actually become, and a year or so passed in such delight as no words can ever describe.

One day his wife said to him, "Would you like to enter into the inner enclosure and see as the fairies see?"

He replied, "Gladly would I."

She then led him into a special park where there were lovely walks, surrounded by green hills. As they advanced there were charming views, with springs of water and sparkling cascades. The scene grew gradually more entrancing, with jewelled flowers and scintillating spray, lovely birds and animals disporting themselves. A man once entering here would never again think of earth as a place to return to.

After seeing this he ascended the highest peak of all, which was like a tower of many stories. Before him lay a wide stretch of sea, with islands of the blessed standing out of the water, and long stretches of pleasant land in view. His wife showed them all to him, pointing out this and that. They seemed filled with golden palaces and surrounded with a halo of light. They were peopled with happy souls, some riding on cranes, some on the phoenix, some on the unicorn; some were sitting on the clouds, some sailing by on the wind, some walking on the air, some gliding gently up the streams, some descending from above, some ascending, some moving west, some north, some gathering in groups. Flutes and harps sounded sweetly. So many and so startling were the things seen that he could never tell the tale of them. After the day had passed they returned.

Thus was their joy unbroken, and when two years had gone by she bore him two sons.

Time moved on, when one day, unexpectedly, as he was seated with his wife, he began to cry and tears soiled his face. She asked in amazement for the cause of it. "I was thinking," said he, "of how a plain countryman living in poverty had thus become the son-in-law of the king of the genii. But in my home is my poor old mother, whom I have not seen for these years; I would so like to see her that my tears flow."

The wife laughed, and said, "Would you really like to see her? Then go, but do not cry." She told her father that her husband would like to go and see his mother. The master called him and gave his permission. The son thought, of course, that he would call many servants and send him in state, but not so. His wife gave him one little bundle and that was all, so he said good-bye to his father-in-law, whose parting word was, "Go now and see your mother, and in a little I shall call for you again."

He sent with him one servant, and so he passed out through the main gateway. There he saw a poor thin horse with a worn rag of a saddle on his back. He looked carefully and found that they were the dead horse and the dead servant, whom he had lost, restored to him. He gave a start, and asked, "How did you come here?"

The servant answered, "I was coming with you on the road when some one caught me away and brought me here. I did not know the reason, but I have been here for a long time."

The man, in great fear, fastened on his bundle and started on his journey. The genie servant brought up the rear, but after a short distance the world of wonder had become transformed into the old weary world again. Here it was with its fogs, and thorn, and precipice. He looked off toward the world of the genii, and it was but a dream. So overcome was he by his feelings that he broke down and cried.

The genie servant said to him when he saw him weeping, "You have been for several years in the abode of the immortals, but you have not yet attained thereto, for you have not yet forgotten the seven things of earth: anger, sorrow, fear, ambition, hate and selfishness. If you once get rid of these there will be no tears for you." On hearing this he stopped his crying, wiped his cheeks, and asked pardon.

When he had gone a mile farther he found himself on the main road. The servant said to him, "You know the way from this point on, so I shall go back," and thus at last the young man reached his home.

He found there an exorcising ceremony in progress. Witches and spirit worshippers had been called and were saying their prayers. The family, seeing the young man come home thus, were all aghast. "It is his ghost," said they. However, they saw in a little that it was really he himself. The mother asked why he had not come home in all that time. She being a very violent woman in disposition, he did not dare to tell her the truth, so he made up something else. The day of his return was the anniversary of his supposed death, and so they had called the witches for a prayer ceremony. Here he opened the bundle that his wife had given him and found four suits of clothes, one for each season.

In about a year after his return home the mother, seeing him alone, made application for the daughter of one of the village *literati*. The man, being timid by nature and afraid of offending his mother, did not dare to refuse, and was therefore married; but there was no joy in it, and the two never looked at each other.

The young man had a friend whom he had known intimately from childhood. After his return the friend came to see him frequently, and they used to spend the nights talking together. In their talks the friend inquired why in all these years he had never come home. The young man then told him what had befallen him in the land of the genii, and how he had been there and had been married. The friend looked at him in wonder, for he seemed just as he had remembered him except in the matter of clothing. This he found on examination was of very strange material, neither grass cloth, silk nor cotton, but different from them all, and yet warm and comfortable. When spring came the spring clothes sufficed, when summer came those for summer, and for autumn and winter each special suit. They were never washed, and yet never became soiled; they never wore out, and always looked fresh and new. The friend was greatly astonished.

Some three years passed when one day there came once more a servant from the master of the genii, bringing his two sons. There were also letters, saying, "Next year the place where you dwell will be destroyed and all the people will become 'fish and meat' for the enemy, therefore follow this messenger and come, all of you."

He told his friend of this and showed him his two sons. The friend, when he saw these children that looked like silk and jade, confessed the matter to the mother also. She, too, gladly agreed, and so they sold out and had a great feast for all the people of the town, and then bade farewell. This was the year 1635. They left and were never heard of again.

The year following was the Manchu invasion, when the village where the young man had lived was all destroyed. To this day young and old in Ka-pyong tell this story.

PRINCESS MAYBLOSSOM

The following tale comes from Marie-Catherine Le Jumel de Barneville, aka Madame d'Aulnoy, a seventeenth-century Baroness of Normandy, and the author of *Les Contes de Fées* (*Tales of Fairies*), the book from which we get the term 'fairy tale'. Translated by Annie Macdonell, the story of Princess Mayblossom has all the markers of a classic in its genre: a king and queen with only one daughter, an evil curse, some kind fairy godmothers, and *even* a tower. Rather than falling into a deep sleep, Princess Mayblossom is doomed to experience only misery until her twenty-first year (an experience that just reminds me a lot of being a teenager). From there, however, things don't always tread a recognizable path, and you can be sure to enjoy some unforeseen twists and turns in Mayblossom's riotous, fairy-filled adventure.

Once upon a time there lived a king and a queen who had had several children born to them. But they all died, and the king and the queen were so sorry, so very sorry, that they could not be comforted. They were very rich, and the one thing they wanted was to have more children. It was five years since the queen's last son had been born, and everybody thought she would not have any more, for she distressed herself so much in thinking of all the little princes who had been so pretty, and who were dead.

At last, however, the queen knew that another child was to be born to her, and all her thoughts, night and day, were of how to preserve the little creature's life, or of the name it would be called by, or its clothes, or of the dolls and the playthings she would give it. A command was sent out, proclaimed by the sound of trumpets, and stuck up in all the public squares, that the best nurses should present themselves before the queen, for she wished to choose one for her infant. So they came from all the four corners of the earth, and there were none but nurses with their babies to be seen. One day then, when the queen was taking the air in a great forest, she sat down, and said to the king: "Sire, call all our nurses together and choose one, for our cows have not milk enough to provide for so many little children." "Very well, my love," said the king. "Come, and let all the nurses be called." So they all came, one after the other, bowing with much respect before the queen. Then they stood up in a row, each with her back against a tree. After they had taken their places, and the king and queen had admired their fresh complexion, their beautiful teeth, and their look of health and strength, a little wheelbarrow was seen coming up, pushed along by two ugly little dwarfs, and in it a hideous creature with crooked feet, her knees touching her chin, with a great hump on her back. In her arms she held a little monkey, which she was nursing, and she was speaking in a jargon they could not understand. She had also come to offer herself as nurse, but the queen drove her away, saying: "Be off, you great ugly thing. You are very ill-bred to come before me with your hideous face, and if you stay another minute I'll have you dragged off." So the sulky creature passed on, muttering aloud, and drawn along by her hideous little dwarfs she went and stuck herself in the hollow of a great tree, from where she could see everything.

The queen thought nothing more about her, and chose an excellent nurse. But as soon as she had named her choice, a horrible serpent, hidden under the grass, stung the nurse's foot, and she fell in a swoon. The queen, much distressed at this accident, cast her eyes on another. Immediately an eagle passed flying by, carrying a tortoise, which he let fall on the poor nurse's head, and broke it in pieces like a glass. The queen, still more distressed, called for a third nurse, who, in her great eagerness to come forward, struck against a bush with great thorns, and put out her eye. "Ah!" cried the queen. "We are indeed unfortunate to-day. I cannot choose a nurse without bringing some ill-luck upon her. I must leave the care of them to my doctor." As she was rising to return to the palace she heard a stifled laugh, and turning round, she saw behind her the wicked hunchback, looking like an ape as she sat with her little imp in the wheelbarrow. There she was, laughing at the whole company, and especially at the queen, who was so angry that she wished to go and beat her, feeling sure she was the cause of the evil chance that had happened to the nurses. But the hunchback, with three strokes of her wand, turned the dwarfs into winged griffins, the wheelbarrow into a chariot of fire, and they all flew away together into the air, uttering threats and horrible cries.

"Alas! my love, we are lost," said the king. "That was the Fairy Carabosse. The wicked creature has hated me ever since I was a little boy on account of a trick I played her, putting sulphur in her broth. Since that time she has been seeking to revenge herself on me." The queen began to cry. "If I had but known her name," she said: "I would have tried to make friends with her. But now I feel as if I should like to die." When the king saw her so distressed, he said: "Come, my love, let us think what we must do," and he gave her his arm to lean on, for she was still trembling from the fright Carabosse had given her. When the king and the queen were in their room they called their councillors, and shut the doors and windows so that nothing might be heard. Then they determined to have all the fairies for a thousand miles round present at the birth of the child. So without delay they despatched couriers, and sent letters by them—beautifully written and most polite letters—asking them to be so good as to be present at the birth of the royal infant, and to say nothing about the matter to anybody. For they trembled lest Carabosse should hear of it, and come and spoil everything. And to reward them for their trouble, they were promised a hongreline* of blue velvet, a skirt of amaranth velvet, and slippers of crimson satin, a pair of little gilden scissors, and a case full of fine needles.

As soon as the messengers had set off, the queen began to work along with her maidens and her servants at all the things she had promised the fairies. She knew of a good many who might be expected, but only five came, and they arrived just at the moment when the little princess was born. So they shut themselves up in the queen's room without delay to name their fairy gifts. The first one endowed her with perfect beauty, the second with wonderful cleverness, the third with the power of singing, and the fourth with that of writing both in prose and verse. When the fifth was opening her mouth to speak, a noise was heard in the chimney like a great stone falling from the top of a steeple, and Carabosse, all covered with soot, made her appearance, screeching out: "Here is my gift to the little one, I wish:—

"That all her youth be overcast
Till her twentieth year be past."

---

* A Hungarian jacket.

At these words the queen who was in bed began to cry, and to beg Carabosse to take pity on the little princess. And all the fairies said: "Alas! sister, take away this curse from her! What has she done to you?" But the ugly fairy growled, and made no answer. So the fifth fairy, who had not yet spoken, tried to mend matters by endowing the child with a long life full of happiness after the period of the curse should have passed by. Carabosse only laughed, and began singing all kinds of mocking songs, climbing out of the palace by the same road she had come. All the fairies were in great consternation, but especially the poor queen. She did not forget, however, to give them what she had promised, adding even ribbons, which they are very fond of, and entertaining them hospitably.

The eldest fairy, as she was going away, said that in her opinion the princess, till she was twenty years old, should be kept in some place where she would see no one but the attendants chosen for her, and where she would be closely guarded. Thereupon the king had a tower built, in which there was not a single window, and where you could not see except by candle light. To get in you had to go through a vault which stretched under the ground for a league, and it was through this passage that everything that the nurses and the governesses wanted was brought. Every twenty paces there were great doors, with strong locks, and all along numerous guards were stationed.

The young princess had been called Mayblossom, for she had a complexion of lilies and roses, fresher and brighter than the spring. In everything she did or said she excelled, learning the most difficult sciences as if they were quite easy. And she grew so tall, and so beautiful, that the king and the queen never saw her without shedding tears of joy. Sometimes she would beg them to stay with her, or to take her away with them, for she wearied in the tower, without knowing why. But they always put it off. Her nurse, who had never left her, and who was not lacking in intelligence, told her sometimes what the world was like, and she understood everything at once just as if she had seen it. The king would often say to the queen: "My love, Carabosse will be made a fool of. We are cleverer than she is, and our Mayblossom will be happy in spite of her predictions." And the queen would laugh till the tears came, to think of the annoyance of the wicked fairy. They had had Mayblossom's portrait painted, and had sent pictures of her throughout the whole world, for the time to release her from the tower being at hand, they wished to marry her. At last, only four days were wanting to complete the twenty years, and the court and the town were very joyous at the thought of the approaching liberty of the princess. And their joy was all the greater when they heard that King Merlin wished to have her for his own, and that he was sending his ambassador, Fanfarinet, to ask her hand in marriage.

The nurse, who told the princess everything, brought her this news, telling her that no sight in the world would be so fine as Fanfarinet's entrance. "Ah, how unfortunate I am!" she cried. "I am shut up here in a dark tower, as if I had committed some great crime. I have never seen the sky, nor the sun, nor the stars, whose wonders are so much talked of. I have never seen a horse, nor a monkey, nor a lion, except in a picture. The king and the queen say they are going to release me when I am twenty years old, but they only say that to make me have patience. I know quite well they wish me to die here, though in nothing have I offended them." Thereupon she began to cry, so long and bitterly that her eyes were as big as her fists; and her nurse, and her foster-sister, and the under-nurse, and the woman who sang her to sleep, and the little nurse-maid, who all loved her passionately, began to weep too so long and bitterly that nothing was heard but sobs and sighs, till they thought they must choke, so great was their distress. When the princess saw them so ready to grieve with her, she took a knife, and said in a loud voice: "There! I am determined to kill myself on the spot, if you do not find some means of letting me see the grand entrance of Fanfarinet. The king and the queen will never know. Choose, therefore, whether you would rather I should kill myself here, or whether you will do what I ask." At these words the nurse and the others began to cry again still louder, and they all determined to let her see Fanfarinet or die themselves in the attempt. The rest of the night they spent in making plans as to how this could be carried out, but in vain; and Mayblossom, who was in despair, said without ceasing: "Never tell me again that you love me. You would find some means if you did, for I have heard that love and friendship can do anything."

At last they came to the conclusion that a hole would have to be made in the tower, on that side of the town by which Fanfarinet would come. So pushing aside the princess's bed, they all set to work day and night without stopping. By means of scraping, they took away first the plaster and then the little stones, till at last they made a hole through which with much difficulty you might have slipped a fine needle. It was through this opening that Mayblossom saw the light for the first time. She was quite dazzled by it. Looking as she did steadily through the little hole, she saw Fanfarinet appear at the head of his whole troop. He was riding on a white horse which danced to the sound of the trumpets, rearing in a splendid fashion. Six flute-players walked in front, playing the finest opera airs, and six hautboys took up the sound. Then the trumpets and the timbrels struck up. Fanfarinet was dressed in a doublet, embroidered with pearls. His boots were of gold, and scarlet plumes waved on his helmet, and ribbons floated from every part of his dress, while he was so covered with diamonds—for King Merlin had whole rooms full of them—that the sun's splendour was as nothing to his. Mayblossom at this sight was beside herself, and quite exhausted. After considering the matter a little, she swore that she would marry none but the beautiful Fanfarinet, that there was no reason for thinking his master would be as beautiful, and she had no ambition to marry one of high rank; that if she had lived happily in a tower, she could live happily, if need be, in some castle in the country with him, and that she would think bread and water in his company better than chicken and sugar-plums with anybody else. In short, she spoke so much that her women could not think where she had learnt a quarter of what she said. When they pleaded her rank and the wrong she would be doing herself, she bade them be silent, and would not deign to listen to their words.

As soon as Fanfarinet had come into the palace of the king, the queen sent for her daughter. All the streets were carpeted, and the ladies stood at the windows, some with baskets full of flowers in their hands, some with baskets full of pearls, others, what were still better, delicious sweetmeats, to throw at her when she passed by. Her maids were just beginning to dress her when there came to the tower a dwarf, mounted on an elephant. He had been sent by the five good fairies who had given her gifts when she was born. They sent her a crown, a sceptre, a dress of gold brocade, a skirt made of butterflies' wings, worked in the most wonderful way, with a still more marvellous casket, full of jewels of priceless value. Never were such treasures seen. At sight of them the queen was speechless with admiration, but the princess looked at them all indifferently, for she was only thinking of Fanfarinet. They thanked the dwarf, and gave him also a pistole to go and drink their health with, and more than a thousand ells of many coloured ribbons, with which he made himself fine garters, and a breast knot, and a rosette for his hat. Being small, when he had put all the ribbons on, you could no longer see him. The queen said she would go and look for something pretty to send back to the fairies, and the princess, who was very kind-hearted, gave them several German spinning-wheels, with distaffs made of cedar-wood.

When they had arrayed the princess in all the rarest things the dwarf had brought, she seemed to everybody so beautiful that the sun hid itself in spite, and the moon, who is never too shamefaced, dared not appear while she was on the road. She walked on foot through the streets over rich carpets, the assembled people in crowds crying around her: "Ah, how beautiful she is! How beautiful she is!" As she walked in her gorgeous robes between the queen and four or five dozen princesses of the blood—not to speak of more than ten dozen who had come from neighbouring states to be present at the feast—the sky began to darken, and the thunder to rumble, and the rain and the hail to fall in torrents. The queen put her royal mantle over her head, and the ladies their skirts. Mayblossom was just going to do the same when the noise of numberless ravens, and screech-owls, carrion-crows, and other birds of evil omen was heard in the air, their croakings boding nothing good. At the same time an ugly owl, of an enormous size, came swooping down, holding in his beak a scarf of spider's web, embroidered with bats' wings. It let this scarf fall on Mayblossom's shoulders, and great bursts of laughter were heard, a sure enough sign that it was some mischievous trick of Carabosse's planning.

At this terrible sight everybody began to cry, and the queen, more distressed than anyone else, wanted to snatch away the black scarf, which seemed, however, to be nailed to her daughter's shoulders. "Ah!" she said, "this is a trick which our enemy has played us. Nothing can appease her. In vain have I sent her fifty pounds of sweetmeats, as much of our own especial sugar, and two Mayence hams. She has taken no notice of them." While she was lamenting thus, they were all getting wet to the skin. Mayblossom, her head full of the ambassador, was speeding on in perfect silence, thinking to herself that provided she pleased him, she did not care either for Carabosse or for her ill-omened scarf. She was wondering that he did not come to meet her, when all at once she saw him by the king's side. Immediately the trumpets, drums, and violins struck up gaily. The cries of the people redoubled, and in fact there were no bounds to the rejoicing.

Fanfarinet was very ready-witted. Yet when he saw the fair Mayblossom with so much grace and dignity, he was so delighted that instead of speaking he only gaped. You would have said he was drunk, though of a truth he had only taken one cup of chocolate. He was in despair at having forgotten in a moment a speech he had been repeating every day for months, and which he knew well enough to be able to say in his sleep. While he was torturing his memory to call back the words, he kept bowing low before the princess, who, for her part, made half-a-dozen curtsies without knowing what she was doing. At last she spoke, and to relieve him from the trouble in which she saw him, she said: "My Lord Fanfarinet, I feel absolutely certain that every thought of yours is charming, for I know you are full of intelligence. But let us make haste and reach the palace. It is pouring in torrents. The wicked Carabosse wants to drown us, but when we are inside we can laugh at her." He answered her with much gallantry, for the fairy had wisely foreseen the fire that the fair eyes of the princess would light, and it was to temper it she poured out this deluge of water. With these few words he gave her his hand to help her on her way, while low in his ear she whispered: "I feel for you what you would never guess, if I did not tell you myself. It is somewhat difficult for me to do so, but 'evil to him that evil thinks'. Know, therefore, my Lord Ambassador, that I admired you very much when I first saw you on your fine, prancing horse, and I felt full of regret that you should come here on another's errand. There is a remedy to be found for this, if your courage is as great as mine. Instead of marrying you in the name of your master, I shall marry you in your own. I know you are not a prince, but you please me just as much as if you were, and we shall flee away together into some corner of the world. At first it will make some talk. But another girl will do as I have done, or perhaps worse; and then they will leave us alone and talk of her, and I shall have the pleasure of living with you."

Fanfarinet thought he must be dreaming, for Mayblossom was so magnificent a princess, that unless by some strange caprice of fortune he could have never hoped for this honour she did him. He had not even strength left to answer her. If they had been alone, he would have thrown himself at her feet. As it was, he took the liberty of wringing her hand so vigorously that he hurt her little finger very much. But she never cried out, so infatuated was she. When she entered the palace all kinds of musical instruments began to play, mingled with voices like those of the angels, so exquisite that no one dared to breathe for fear of making too much noise. After the king had kissed his daughter on the forehead and on the two cheeks, he said to her: "My little lambkin (for he gave her all kind of pet names), will you not be glad to marry the son of the great King Merlin? Here is Lord Fanfarinet, who will perform the ceremony for him, and who will take you away into the finest kingdom in the world." "Yes, my father," she said, with a low bow; "I am willing to do anything to please you, provided my good mother gives her consent." "Yes, I give my consent, my darling," said the queen, embracing her. "Come now, let the tables be spread." And this was done in haste. There were a hundred spread in a great gallery, and in the memory of man never was there such feasting. Only Mayblossom and Fanfarinet did not partake, for they only thought of looking at each other, until they became so dreamy that they forgot all that was going on around them. After the feast there was a ball, a ballet, and a play acted, but it was already so late, and everybody had eaten so much, that in spite of all their efforts, the people were sleeping on their feet. The king and the queen, overcome also with sleep, threw themselves on a sofa. The greater part of the dames and cavaliers were snoring, the musicians played out of tune, and the players did not know what they were saying. Only our lovers were wide awake as mice, and looking at each other with soft looks. The princess, seeing that there was nothing to fear, and that the guards lying on their pallets were asleep too, said to Fanfarinet: "Trust me, let us take advantage of so favourable an opportunity, for if I wait for the wedding ceremony the king will give me waiting women and a prince to accompany me to your King Merlin. We had better go now, as quickly as we can."

Getting up, she took the king's dagger, which was studded with diamonds, and the head-dress which the queen had taken off that she might sleep more at her ease. She gave her white hand to Fanfarinet, and as he took it he knelt on the ground and said: "I swear to be for ever faithful and obedient to your highness. Great princess, you do everything for me. What would I not do for you!" They left the palace, the ambassador carrying a dark lantern in his hand, and through very muddy streets they reached the port, where they got into a little boat. There was a poor old boatman in it asleep. They awoke him, and when he saw

Mayblossom so beautiful and so gaily dressed, with so many diamonds, and with her spider-web scarf, he took her for the Goddess of Night, and knelt before her. But as there was no time to be lost, she ordered him to set off. It was very venturesome, for neither moon nor stars could be seen, and the air was still full of the storm which Carabosse had caused. It is true there was a carbuncle in the queen's head-dress which shone brighter than fifty lighted torches, and Fanfarinet, indeed, might have done without the dark lantern, the carbuncle having the power of making them invisible. Fanfarinet asked the princess where she would like to go. "Alas!" she said, "I wish to go with you. That is all I care for." "But, madam," he answered; "I dare not take you to King Merlin's court, for there I should be killed like a dog." "Very well," she answered; "let us go to the desert Isle of Squirrels. It is far enough away, so we shall not be followed." Then she ordered the sailor to set off, and though it was only a little boat, he obeyed.

When day was dawning the first thought of the king, the queen, and of everybody, after they had shaken themselves a little and rubbed their eyes, was to complete the princess's marriage ceremony. The queen, in great haste, asked for her grand head-dress to put on her hair. They looked for it everywhere, from cabinets even to saucepans, but it was not to be found. The queen, very anxious, ran up and down stairs, to the cellar, to the attic, everywhere, but it was nowhere to be seen.

The king, for his part, wished to array himself with his magnificent dagger, and in the same way they began to rummage everywhere, opening boxes and caskets, the keys of which had been lost for more than a hundred years. They found all kinds of curious things, dolls that moved their heads and their eyes, golden sheep with their little lambs, lemon peel, pickled walnuts, but none of these made up to the king for his loss. He was so desperate that he tore his beard, and the queen, for company, tore her hair, for in truth the head-dress and the dagger were worth more than ten towns as large as Madrid.

When the king saw there was no hope of finding either of them, he said to the queen: "My love, take courage, and let us haste to complete the ceremony which already has cost us so dear". When he asked where the princess was, her nurse came forward and said: "Your majesty, I assure you that I have looked for her for more than two hours, and I cannot find her". These words brought the king and queen's grief to a climax, and the queen began to cry like an eagle whose little ones have been taken away, and fell down in a faint. You never saw such a pitiful sight, and they had to throw more than two buckets of Queen-of-Hungary water on her majesty's face before she came to herself. The court ladies and the maids of honour wept, and all the valets cried out: "What! is the king's daughter really lost?" The king seeing that the princess was not to be found, said to his chief page: "Go and fetch Fanfarinet, who is sleeping in some corner, that he may come and mourn with us". So the page went about looking everywhere for Fanfarinet, but he was no more to be found than were Mayblossom, the head-dress, and the dagger. This was another addition to their troubles, and their majesties were in despair.

The king called all his councillors and men-at-arms together, and went with the queen into the great hall, which had already been hung with black. They had put off their gay dresses, and they each wore a long mourning robe, tied round the waist with a cord. When their people saw them in this condition, there was no heart so hard but was ready to break, and the hall resounded with sobs and sighs, while streams of tears flowed over the floor. As the king had had no time to prepare his speech he was three hours before he could say a word. At last he began:—

"Listen now, gentle and simple. I have lost my dear daughter, Mayblossom. I do not know whether she has melted away or whether she has been stolen away from me. The queen's head-dress and my dagger, which are worth their weight in gold, have also disappeared, and what is worse, the ambassador Fanfarinet is no longer to be found. I very much fear that the king, his master, receiving no news, will come and seek for him at our court, and that he will accuse us of cutting him to pieces. I should be more patient if I had any money, but I must own to you that the expenses of the wedding have ruined me. Counsel me, therefore, my dear subjects, as to what I can do to get back my daughter, Fanfarinet, and the property I have lost."

Everyone admired the king's fine speech: he had never spoken so well before. Lord Gambille, the chancellor of the kingdom, then spoke:—

"Your majesty, we regret very much the trouble that has befallen you, and we would have given you our very wives and our little ones, so that you might have less reason to grieve. But evidently all this has been brought about by the Fairy Carabosse. The princess's twenty years had not yet been completed, and since I must speak frankly, I ought to tell you that I noticed she was always looking at Fanfarinet, and he was always looking at her too.

So perhaps Love has been playing some of his tricks."

At these words the queen, who was very quick-tempered, interrupted him. "Take care what you are saying, my Lord Gambille. The princess would not be disposed to fall in love with Fanfarinet. I have brought her up too well." Thereupon the nurse, who was listening to everything, came and knelt before the king and queen. "I come to confess to you what has happened," she said. "The princess declared she must see Fanfarinet, or die, so we made a little hole, through which she saw him, and at once she swore she would never marry anyone else." On hearing this everyone was in great distress, for they knew well that Chancellor Gambille was a very keen-sighted man. The queen in great wrath scolded the nurse, the foster-sister, the under-nurse, the woman who had used to sing the princess to sleep, and the little nursemaid, so soundly that they all but died under her reproaches.

Then Admiral Chapeau-Pointu, interrupting the queen, cried out: "Come, let us go after Fanfarinet. There can be no doubt but this rascal has run away with our princess." Everybody clapped their hands at this, saying: "Let us go!" Some embarked by sea, others went by land from kingdom to kingdom, beating drums, and sounding trumpets, and when people gathered round them, they would cry: "Whoever wants to gain a beautiful doll, pots of preserves (dry or liquid), a pair of scissors, a gilded robe, a fine satin cap, has only to tell us where the Princess Mayblossom is who was stolen away by Fanfarinet." But every man answered: "Go elsewhere, we have not seen them". Those who pursued the princess by sea were more fortunate, for after sailing for a long time they saw one night something shining before them like a great fire. They dared not come near it, not knowing what it might be, but all at once this light seemed to land on the desert Isle of Squirrels.

In truth it was no other than the princess and her lover, and it was the carbuncle they had seen shining. Mayblossom and Fanfarinet disembarked, and after having given a hundred golden crowns to the good man who had brought them, they bade him farewell, making him swear by the eyes in his head to speak of nothing he had seen or heard. The first thing the boatman met was the king's vessels, which he had no sooner recognised than he tried to avoid. But the admiral sent a boat after him, and the good man was so aged and so weak that he had not strength to row fast enough. So coming up with him they brought him before the admiral, who had him searched. They found on him a hundred gold crowns quite new, for they had coined money for the princess's wedding-feast. The admiral questioned him, and so as not to be obliged to answer, he pretended he was deaf and dumb. "Very well," said the admiral, "tie this dumb man to the great mast, and give him a flogging. That is the best cure of all for the dumb." When the old man saw that he meant this, he confessed that a girl, more like an angel than a human creature, and a beautiful knight, had ordered him to take them to the desert Isle of Squirrels. Hearing this the admiral knew it must be the princess, and he sent his fleet to surround the island.

Meanwhile Mayblossom tired out by the sea, having found a green lawn under the shade of thick trees, lay down and fell quietly asleep. But Fanfarinet whose hunger was keener than his love, did not leave her long in peace. "Do you think, madam," he said, waking her up, "that I can remain long here? I see nothing to eat. Even were you fairer than the dawn, that hardly would suffice, for one must eat. My teeth are very long, and my stomach very empty." "What, Fanfarinet," she answered, "does not the affection I feel for you stand you in stead of everything? Is your mind not filled with your good fortune?" "With my misfortunes, rather," he cried.

"I would to heaven you were still in your black tower!" "Sir Knight," she said, graciously, "I beg you, do not be angry. I shall go and search everywhere, and perhaps I may find some fruit." "I wish," he answered, "that you would find a wolf to eat you up!" The princess, in great distress, ran through the woods, tearing her pretty clothes with the briars, and her white skin with the thorns till she was all full of scratches as if she had been playing with cats. See what it is to fall in love—only trouble comes of it. After having searched everywhere, she came back very sad to Fanfarinet, to tell him she had found nothing, but he turned his back on her, and went away muttering. Next day they searched again, but still all in vain, so that they were three days without eating anything but leaves and some cockchafers. The princess made no complaint, though she was very delicate. "I would not mind," she said, "if I suffered by myself, and I should not care though I died of hunger, provided you had enough to eat." "It would be all the same to me," he answered, "whether you died or not, provided I had what I want." "Is it possible," she asked, "that my death would make so little difference to you? Are these the oaths you made me?" "There is a great difference," he answered, "between a man when he is comfortable, and neither hungry nor thirsty, and an unfortunate wretch like to die on a desert island." "I am in the same danger," she said, "and I make no complaint." "It would ill become you to do so," he replied, harshly. "You wished to leave your father and mother, and go gadding up and down. Well, here we are, in a nice place too!" "But it was for love of you, Fanfarinet," she said, holding out her hand. "I could have done without that," he answered, and then he turned his back on her.

The beautiful princess, overcome with grief, began to cry so bitterly that she would have moved a stone to pity. She sat down near a bush covered with red and white roses. After having looked at them for some time, she said: "How happy you are, young flowers. The zephyrs caress you, the dew moistens you, the sun brings you beauty, the bees love you, the thorns defend you. Everybody admires you. Alas! why should you be happier than I?" At these thoughts she shed so many tears that the root of the rose tree was quite wet. Then she was much astonished to see that the bush was moving, and the roses opening out, and that the fairest of them all said: "If you had not fallen in love, your lot would be as desirable as mine. Whoever loves is exposed to the utmost dangers. Poor princess, take the honeycomb you will find in the hollow of yonder tree. But do not be so foolish as to give it to Fanfarinet." Off she ran to the tree, not knowing yet whether she was dreaming or whether she was really awake. She found the honey, and as soon as she had done so, she took it to her ungrateful lover. "Here," she said, "is a honeycomb. If I had liked I might have eaten it all by myself, but I would rather share it with you." Without a word of thanks, without even a look, he tore it out of her hands, and ate the whole of it, refusing to give her one little morsel, even adding mockery to his cruelty, saying it was too sweet, that it would spoil her teeth, and a hundred other like taunts.

Mayblossom, still more distressed, sat down below an oak, and spoke to it very much as she had done to the rose tree. The oak, moved with pity, lowered some of its branches and said: "It would be a pity were you to die, Mayblossom. Take this pitcher of milk and drink it, and don't give a drop to that ungrateful lover of yours." The princess, very much astonished, looked behind and saw a large pitcher of milk. Her only thought at the moment was of Fanfarinet's thirst after having eaten more than fifteen pounds of honey, and she ran with her pitcher to him. "Drink, my beautiful Fanfarinet," she said, "and don't forget to leave me some, for I am dying of hunger and thirst." But he snatched it roughly from her, drank all the milk up at a single draught, then throwing the pitcher on the stones, broke it in pieces, saying, with a mocking smile: "Those who have eaten nothing are not thirsty". The princess clasped her hands, and lifting her beautiful eyes to heaven, she said: "I have deserved it. It is a punishment for having so rashly fallen in love with a man whom I did not know, for having run away with him, forgetting my rank, and the misfortune with which Carabosse threatened me." Then she began to cry again, more bitterly than ever she had done in her life, and plunging into the thickest part of the wood, she fell down from sheer weakness at the foot of an elm tree, on which a nightingale was perched and singing beautifully. Shaking his wings he sang these words as if only for Mayblossom's benefit. He had learnt them out of Ovid on purpose:—

"Love is a traitor, then beware his guile;
For all his favours doth he ask a price;
Most full of danger when they most entice;
Deadliest the poison in his sweetest smile."

"Who can know that better than I do?" she cried, interrupting her. "Alas! I know only too well the sharpness of his arrows and the hardness of my lot." "Take courage," said the tender nightingale; "and search in this bush. You will find sugar-plums and tarts, but do not be so foolish as to give any to Fanfarinet." The princess had no need of this warning to keep them for herself. She had not yet forgotten the two last tricks he had played her, and besides, she was in great want of food, so she munched the sugar-plums and the tarts all by herself. Greedy Fanfarinet, seeing her eating without him, flew into such a temper that he ran towards her, his eyes flashing with anger, and his sword in his hand to kill her. In a moment she had uncovered the stone on her headdress, which made her invisible, and going farther off she reproached him with his ingratitude, but in such a way as made him understand well enough that she could not yet bring herself to hate him.

Meanwhile Admiral Chapeau-Pointu had despatched John Caquet, courier-in-ordinary to the council, with his straw boots, to tell the king that the princess and Fanfarinet had landed in the Island of Squirrels, but that, not knowing the country, he feared there might be ambuscades. This news gave great satisfaction to their majesties, and the king sent for a great book, each leaf of which was eight ells in length. It was the masterpiece of a learned fairy, and in it was a description of the whole earth. He found from this book that the Isle of Squirrels was not inhabited. "Go," he said, therefore, to John Caquet, "and command the admiral on my behalf to land at once. He may well be very impatient at the thought of leaving my daughter so long with Fanfarinet, and at all events I am." As soon as John Caquet had reached the fleet, the admiral ordered the drums to beat, and the timbals and the trumpets to sound. Hautboys, flutes, violins, hurdy-gurdies, organs, guitars struck up. What a desperate noise they made! for every instrument of war or peace was heard throughout the whole island. At this noise the princess, in alarm, ran towards her lover to offer him help. He was not brave, and their common terror very quickly reconciled them. "Keep behind me," she said. "I shall walk in front, and uncovering the invisible stone, I shall take my father's dagger and kill a part of our enemies while you kill the others with your sword." So the invisible princess stepped forward amidst the soldiers, and she and Fanfarinet killed them all without being seen. Nothing was heard but cries of "I am dead!" "I am dying!" It was in vain the soldiers drew their swords, they could touch nothing, for the princess and her lover ducked down every time, and the blows passed over their heads. At last the admiral, in great trouble at losing so many men in such an extraordinary way, without knowing who were their assailants, nor how to defend himself, beat a retreat, and returned to his ship to hold a council.

The night being already far advanced, the princess and Fanfarinet took refuge in the thickest part of the wood. She was so tired that she lay down on the grass, and was just falling asleep when she heard a little soft voice whispering in her ear: "Run, Mayblossom, for Fanfarinet is going to kill and eat you". Quickly opening her eyes, she saw by the light of the carbuncle the wicked Fanfarinet's arm raised ready to plunge his sword into her bosom. For seeing how plump and white she was, and being very hungry, he wished to kill and eat her. She did not hesitate long as to what she should do, but quietly drawing her dagger, which she had kept ever since the battle, she stabbed him so furiously in the eye that he died on the spot. "There, you ungrateful wretch," she cried, "take this last favour from my hands, the one you have best deserved! Be an example to all false lovers in time to come; and may your faithless soul never rest in peace!"

When the first heat of her anger was past, and she thought of her situation, she was nearly as lifeless as he whom she had just killed. "What will become of me?" she cried, weeping. "I am all alone in this island. Wild beasts will come and devour me, or I shall die of hunger." She was almost sorry she had not allowed Fanfarinet to eat her. All of a tremble she sat down, waiting and longing for the light, for she was afraid of ghosts, and especially of goblins. She was leaning against a tree, peering through the darkness, when she saw on one side a grand golden chariot, drawn by six great, tufted hens. The coachman was a cock, and the postillion a fat chicken. In the chariot there was a lady, so very, very beautiful, that she seemed like the sun. Her dress was all embroidered with gold spangles and silver bars. And another chariot she saw, to which six bats were harnessed. The coachman was a raven, and the postillion a blackbeetle. And in this chariot was a hideous little monster, dressed in serpentskin, and on her head for a top knot was a great toad. Never, never was anyone so astonished as the young princess. As she was looking at these wonders, she saw the chariots advance suddenly to meet each other, and the fair lady holding a golden lance, the hideous imp a rusty pike, they began a stern combat, which lasted more than a quarter of an hour. At last the beautiful lady was victorious, and the ugly one flew away with her bats. At that moment the beauty stepped down on the ground and addressed Mayblossom.

"Do not fear, dear princess," she said, "that I have come here for any other reason than to do you a service. The combat I have had with Carabosse was all for love of you. She wished to have authority to beat you because you came out of the tower four days before the twenty years. But you saw how I took your part, and that I chased her away. Enjoy the happiness therefore which I have gained for you." The grateful princess fell down before her. "Great Queen of the Fairies," she said, "your generosity delights me. I do not know how to thank you, but I feel that there is not a drop of the blood which you have just saved which is not at your service." The fairy kissed her three times, and made her still more beautiful than she had been before—if that were possible. She ordered the cock to go to the king's ships, and to tell the admiral he might come without fear. Then she sent the fat chicken to her palace, to fetch the most beautiful dresses in the world for Mayblossom. The admiral hearing the cock's news, was so delighted that he nearly died of joy. He hastened to the isle with his men, and even John Caquet seeing how everyone hurried as they landed from the ships, hurried too, like the others, bearing on his shoulder a spit loaded with game. Hardly had Admiral Chapeau-Pointu gone a league when he saw on the high road the chariot and the hens, and the two ladies in it. He recognised the princess, and went and flung himself at her feet, but she said that all the honour was due to the generous fairy, who had saved her from the clutches of Carabosse. So he made her the prettiest speech that was ever spoken on a like occasion. While he was talking, the fairy interrupted him, crying: "I swear I smell roast beef". "Yes, madam," answered John Caquet, showing the spit laden with the fine birds. "If your highness would but taste them?" "Very willingly," she said, "but less for my own sake than for the princess's, who is in much need of a good meal." So they sent off at once to the ships for all that was necessary, and the joy of having found the princess again, added to the good cheer, left nothing to wish for.

The repast being over, and the fat chicken come back, the fairy dressed Mayblossom in a dress of green and gold brocade, sprinkled with rubies and pearls. She tied her fair hair with cords of diamonds and emeralds, and crowned her with flowers, and when she made her get into her chariot, all the stars that saw her passing thought it was the dawn that had not yet disappeared, and they greeted her in passing with: "All hail! Aurora".

After the fairy and the princess had bidden each other a tender farewell Mayblossom said: "And, madam, shall I not tell the queen, my mother, who has done me all this kindness?" "Fair princess," she answered, "kiss her for me, and tell her I am the fifth fairy who brought you a gift at your birth." When the princess was in the vessel they fired all the guns, and sent off endless rockets. She reached port quite safely, and found the king and queen waiting for her ready to greet her with so much kindness that they gave her no time to ask them to forgive her foolish conduct in the past, though she meant to throw herself at their feet as soon as she had seen them. But the tenderness of her parents prevented her, and they put all the blame on old Carabosse.

Just at that moment the son of the great king arrived, anxious at not having received any news from his ambassador. He had a thousand horses, and thirty lackeys gaily dressed in red with fine gold braid, and he was a hundred times lovelier than the false Fanfarinet. They took care not to tell him the story of the princess's adventures, for that might have made him somewhat suspicious. They told him very gravely that his ambassador being thirsty, and going to draw water to drink, had fallen into the well and got drowned. He had no difficulty in believing this, and the marriage was celebrated amidst joy so great as to blot out entirely the remembrance of past sorrows.

HILDUR, THE QUEEN OF THE ELVES

The story of 'Hildur, Queen of the Elves' comes from *Icelandic Legends*, a collection of folk-tales compiled by nineteenth-century folklorist Jón Árnason, who is often credited with publishing the first ever collection of Icelandic folk-tales – a contribution this volume gratefully acknowledges. Translated here by George E. J. Powell and Eiríkur Magnússon, Hildur's story is one that features a popular figure of Icelandic, and more widely Nordic, folklore and mythology: the elf. The elves (álfar) of Iceland are known as the Hidden People (Huldufólk), due in part to their existence in a realm parallel to our own that is hidden to most. This is the wondrous yet dangerous realm that Árnason's Queen Hildur rules over and in which our next curious mortal protagonist unexpectedly finds himself.

Once, in a mountainous district, there lived a certain farmer, whose name and that of his farm have not been handed down to us; so we cannot tell them. He was unmarried, and had a housekeeper named Hildur, concerning whose family and descent he knew nothing whatever. She had all the indoor affairs of the farm under her charge, and managed them wondrous well. All the inmates of the house, the farmer himself to boot, were fond of her, as she was clean and thrifty in her habits, and kind and gentle in speech.

Everything about the place flourished exceedingly, but the farmer always found the greatest difficulty in hiring a herdsman; a very important matter, as the well-being of the farm depended not a little on the care taken of the sheep. This difficulty did not arise from any fault of the farmer's own, or from neglect on the part of the housekeeper to the comforts of the servants, but from the fact, that no herdsman who entered his service lived more than a year, each one being without fail found dead in his bed, on the morning of Christmas-day. No wonder, therefore, the farmer found herdsmen scarce.

In those times it was the custom of the country to spend the night of Christmas-eve at church, and this occasion for service was looked upon as a very solemn one. But so far was this farm from the church, that the herdsmen, who did not return from their flocks till late in the evening, were unable to go to it on that night until long after the usual time; and as for Hildur, she always remained behind to take care of the house, and always had so much to do in the way of cleaning the rooms and dealing out the rations for the servants, that the family used to come home from church and go to bed long before she had finished her work, and was able to go to bed herself.

The more the reports of the death of herdsman after herdsman, on the night of Christmas-eve, were spread abroad, the greater became the difficulty the farmer found in hiring one, although it was never supposed for an instant that violence was used towards the men, as no mark had ever been found on their bodies; and as, moreover, there was no one to suspect. At length the farmer declared that his conscience would no longer let him thus hire men only in order that they might die, so he determined in future to let luck take care of his sheep, or the sheep take care of themselves.

Not long after he had made this determination, a bold and hardy-looking man came to him and made him a proffer of his services. The farmer said:

"My good friend, I am not in so great need of your services as to hire you."

Then the man asked him, "Have you, then, taken a herdsman for this winter?"

The farmer said, "No; for I suppose you know what a terrible fate has hitherto befallen every one I have hired."

"I have heard of it," said the other, "but the fear of it shall neither trouble me nor prevent my keeping your sheep this winter for you, if you will but make up your mind to take me."

But the farmer would not hear of it at first; "For," said he, "it is a pity, indeed, that so fine a fellow as you should lose your chance of life. Begone, if you are wise, and get work elsewhere."

Yet still the man declared, again and again, that he cared not a whit for the terrors of Christmas-eve, and still urged the farmer to hire him.

At length the farmer consented, in answer to the man's urgent prayer, to take him as herdsman; and very well they agreed together. For everyone, both high and low, liked the man, as he was honest and open, zealous in everything he laid his hands to, and willing to do anyone a good turn, if need were.

On Christmas-eve, towards nightfall, the farmer and all his family went (as has been before declared to be the custom) to church, except Hildur, who remained behind to look after household matters, and the herdsman, who could not leave his sheep in time. Late in the evening, the latter as usual returned home, and after having eaten his supper, went to bed. As soon as he was well between the sheets, the remembrance struck him of what had befallen all the former herdsmen in his position on the same evening, and he thought it would be the best plan for him to lie awake and thus to be ready for any accident, though he was mighty little troubled with fear. Quite late at night, he heard the farmer and his family return from church, enter the house, and having taken supper, go to bed. Still, nothing happened, except that whenever he closed his eyes for a moment, a strange and deadly faintness stole over him, which only acted as one reason the more for his doing his best to keep awake.

Shortly after he had become aware of these feelings, he heard some one creep stealthily up to the side of his bed, and looking through the gloom at the figure, fancied he recognized Hildur the housekeeper. So he feigned to be fast asleep, and felt her place something in his mouth, which he knew instantly to be the bit of a magic bridle, but yet allowed her to fix it on him, without moving. When she had fastened the bridle, she dragged him from his bed with it, and out of the farmhouse, without his being either able or willing to make the least resistance, Then mounting on his back, she made him rise from the ground as if on wings, and rode him through the air, till they arrived at a huge and awful precipice, which yawned, like a great well, down into the earth.

She dismounted at a large stone, and fastening the reins to it, leaped into the precipice. But the herdsman, objecting strongly to being tied to this stone all night, and thinking to himself that it would be no bad thing to know what became of the woman, tried to escape, bridle and all, from the stone. This he found, however, to be impossible, for as long as the bit was in his mouth, he was quite powerless to get away. So he managed, after a short struggle, to get the bridle off his head, and having so done, leapt into the precipice, down which he had seen Hildur disappear. After sinking for a long, long time, he caught a glimpse of Hildur beneath him, and at last they came to some beautiful green meadows.

From all this, the man guessed that Hildur was by no means a common mortal, as she had before made believe to be, and feared if he were to follow her along these green fields, and she turn round and catch sight of him, he might, not unlikely, pay for his curiosity with his life. So he took a magic stone which he always carried about him, the nature of which was to make him invisible when he held it in his palm, and placing it in the hollow of his hand, ran after her with all his strength.

When they had gone some way along the meadows, a splendid palace rose before them, with the way to which Hildur seemed perfectly well acquainted. At her approach a great crowd of people came forth from the doors, and saluted Hildur with respect and joy. Foremost of these walked a man of kingly and noble aspect, whose salutation seemed to be that of a lover or a husband: all the rest bowed to her as if she were their queen. This man was accompanied by two children, who ran up to Hildur, calling her mother, and embraced her. After the people had welcomed their queen, they all returned to the palace, where they dressed her in royal robes, and loaded her hands with costly rings and bracelets.

The herdsman followed the crowd, and posted himself where he would be least in the way of the company, but where he could catch sight easily of all that passed, and lose nothing. So gorgeous and dazzling were the hangings of the hall, and the silver and golden vessels on the table, that he thought he had never, in all his life before, seen the like; not to mention the wonderful dishes and wines which seemed plentiful there, and which, only by the look of them, filled his mouth with water, while he would much rather have filled it with something else.

After he had waited a little time, Hildur appeared in the hall, and all the assembled guests were begged to take their seats, while Hildur sat on her throne beside the king; after which all the people of the court ranged themselves on each side of the royal couple, and the feast commenced.

When it was concluded, the various guests amused themselves, some by dancing, some by singing, others by drinking and revel; but the king and queen talked together, and seemed to the herdsman to be very sad.

While they were thus conversing, three children, younger than those the man had seen before, ran in, and clung round the neck of their mother. Hildur received them with all a mother's love, and, as the youngest was restless, put it on the ground and gave it one of her rings to play with.

After the little one had played a while with the

ring he lost it, and it rolled along the floor towards the herdsman, who, being invisible, picked it up without being perceived, and put it carefully into his pocket. Of course all search for it by the guests was in vain.

When the night was far advanced, Hildur made preparations for departure, at which all the people assembled showed great sorrow, and begged her to remain longer.

The herdsman had observed, that in one corner of the hall sat an old and ugly woman, who had neither received the queen with joy nor pressed her to stay longer.

As soon as the king perceived that Hildur addressed herself to her journey, and that neither his entreaties nor those of the assembly could induce her to stay, he went up to the old woman, and said to her:

"Mother, rid us now of thy curse; cause no longer my queen to live apart and afar from me. Surely her short and rare visits are more pain to me than joy."

The old woman answered him with a wrathful face.

"Never will I depart from what I have said. My words shall hold true in all their force, and on no condition will I abolish my curse."

On this the king turned from her, and going up to his wife, entreated her in the fondest and most loving terms not to depart from him.

The queen answered, "The infernal power of thy mother's curse forces me to go, and perchance this may be the last time that I shall see thee. For lying, as I do, under this horrible ban, it is not possible that my constant murders can remain much longer secret, and then I must suffer the full penalty of crimes which I have committed against my will."

While she was thus speaking the herdsman sped from the palace and across the fields to the precipice, up which he mounted as rapidly as he had come down, thanks to the magic stone.

When he arrived at the rock he put the stone into his pocket, and the bridle over his head again, and awaited the coming of the elf-queen. He had not long to wait, for very soon afterwards Hildur came up through the abyss, and mounted on his back, and off they flew again to the farmhouse, where Hildur, taking the bridle from his head, placed him again in his bed, and retired to her own. The herdsman, who by this time was well tired out, now considered it safe to go to sleep, which he did, so soundly as not to wake till quite late on Christmas-morning.

Early that same day the farmer rose, agitated and filled with the fear that, instead of passing Christmas in joy, he should assuredly, as he so often had before, find his herdsman dead, and pass it in sorrow and mourning. So he and all the rest of the family went to the bedside of the herdsman.

When the farmer had looked at him and found him breathing, he praised God aloud for his mercy in preserving the man from death.

Not long afterwards the man himself awoke and got up.

Wondering at his strange preservation the farmer asked him how he had passed the night, and whether he had seen or heard anything.

The man replied, "No; but I have had a very curious dream."

"What was it?" asked the farmer.

Upon which the man related everything that had passed in the night, circumstance for circumstance, and word for word, as well as he could remember. When he had finished his story every one was silent for wonder, except Hildur, who went up to him and said:

"I declare you to be a liar in all that you have said, unless you can prove it by sure evidence."

Not in the least abashed, the herdsman took from his pocket the ring which he had picked up on the floor of the hall in Elf-land, and showing it to her said:

"Though my dream needs no proof, yet here is one you will not doubtless deem other than a sure one; for is not this your gold ring, Queen Hildur?"

Hildur answered, "It is, no doubt, my ring. Happy man! may you prosper in all you undertake, for you have released me from the awful yoke which my mother-in-law laid, in her wrath, upon me, and from the curse of a yearly murder."

And then Hildur told them the story of her life as follows:—

"I was born of an obscure family among the elves. Our king fell in love with me and married me, in spite of the strong disapproval of his mother. She swore eternal hatred to me in her anger against her son, and said to him, 'Short shall be your joy with this fair wife of yours, for you shall see her but once a year, and that only at the expense of a murder. This is my curse upon her, and it shall be carried out to the letter. She shall go and serve in the upper world, this queen, and every Christmas-eve shall ride a man, one of her fellow-servants, with this magic bridle, to the confines of Elf-land, where she shall pass a few hours with you, and then ride him back again till his very heart breaks with toil, and his very life leaves him. Let her thus enjoy her queenship.'

"And this horrible fate was to cling to me until I should either have these murders brought home to me, and be condemned to death, or should meet with a gallant man, like this herdsman, who should have nerve and courage to follow me down into Elf-land, and be able to prove afterwards that he had been there with me, and seen the customs of my people. And now I must confess that all the former herdsmen were slain by me, but no penalty shall touch me for their murders, as I committed them against my will. And as for you, O courageous man, who have dared, the first of human beings, to explore the realms of Elf-land, and have freed me from the yoke of this awful curse, I will reward you in times to come, but not now.

"A deep longing for my home and my loved ones impels me hence. Farewell!"

With these words Hildur vanished from the sight of the astonished people, and was never seen again.

But our friend the herdsman, leaving the service of the farmer, built a farm for himself, and prospered, and became one of the chief men in the country, and always ascribed, with grateful thanks, his prosperity to Hildur, Queen of the Elves.

RHIANNON

The next story is but one excerpt from the anonymously authored medieval Welsh epic known as the *Mabinogion* (it's also one of my personal favourites). The *Mabinogion* itself is the earliest piece of surviving prose from Britain and features countless legends that include such well-known figures as King Arthur. Here we have the first complete translation of the Old Welsh into English courtesy of Lady Charlotte Guest, which was published between 1838 and 1845. In this particular portion of the text, we follow the hero Pwyll and the otherworldly woman Rhiannon, whose name means 'divine queen' in Welsh and may derive from an earlier British deity known as Rigantona in Brittonic. Rhiannon is fairy, queen, goddess all wrapped up in one, and here we follow her introduction to the mortal Pwyll and their tumultuous journey to getting married, although neither of their stories end here.

Once upon a time, Pwyll was at Narberth his chief palace, where a feast had been prepared for him, and with him was a great host of men. And after the first meal, Pwyll arose to walk, and he went to the top of a mound that was above the palace, and was called Gorsedd Arberth. "Lord," said one of the Court, "it is peculiar to the mound that whosoever sits upon it cannot go thence, without either receiving wounds or blows, or else seeing a wonder." "I fear not to receive wounds and blows in the midst of such a host as this, but as to the wonder, gladly would I see it. I will go therefore and sit upon the mound."

And upon the mound he sat. And while he sat there, they saw a lady, on a pure white horse of large size, with a garment of shining gold around her, coming along the highway that led from the mound; and the horse seemed to move at a slow and even pace, and to be coming up towards the mound. "My men," said Pwyll, "is there any among you who knows yonder lady?" "There is not, Lord," said they. "Go one of you and meet her, that we may know who she is." And one of them arose, and as he came upon the road to meet her, she passed by, and he followed as fast as he could, being on foot; and the greater was his speed, the further was she from him. And when he saw that it profited him nothing to follow her, he returned to Pwyll, and said unto him, "Lord, it is idle for any one in the world to follow her on foot." "Verily," said Pwyll, "go unto the palace, and take the fleetest horse that thou seest, and go after her."

And he took a horse and went forward. And he came to an open level plain, and put spurs to his horse; and the more he urged his horse, the further was she from him. Yet she held the same pace as at first. And his horse began to fail; and when his horse's feet failed him, he returned to the place where Pwyll was. "Lord," said he, "it will avail nothing for any one to follow yonder lady. I know of no horse in these realms swifter than this, and it availed me not to pursue her." "Of a truth," said Pwyll, "there must be some illusion here. Let us go towards the palace." So to the palace they went, and they spent that day. And the next day they arose, and that also they spent until it was time to go to meat. And after the first meal, "Verily," said Pwyll, "we will go the same party as yesterday to the top of the mound. And do thou," said he to one of his young men, "take the swiftest horse that thou knowest in the field." And thus did the young man. And they went towards the mound, taking the horse with them. And as they were sitting down they beheld the lady on the same horse, and in the same apparel, coming along the same road. "Behold," said Pwyll, "here is the lady of yesterday. Make ready, youth, to learn who she is." "My lord," said he, "that will I gladly do." And thereupon the lady came opposite to them. So the youth mounted his horse; and before he had settled himself in his saddle, she passed by, and there was a clear space between them. But her speed was no greater than it had been the day before. Then he put his horse into an amble, and thought that notwithstanding the gentle pace at which his horse went, he should soon overtake her. But this availed him not; so he gave his horse the reins. And still he came no nearer to her than when he went at a foot's pace. And the more he urged his horse, the further was she from him. Yet she rode not faster than before. When he saw that it availed not to follow her, he returned to the place where Pwyll was. "Lord," said he, "the horse can no more than thou hast seen." "I see indeed that it avails not that any one should follow her. And by Heaven," said he, "she must needs have an errand to some one in this plain, if her haste would allow her to declare it. Let us go back to the palace." And to the palace they went, and they spent that night in songs and feasting, as it pleased them.

And the next day they amused themselves until it was time to go to meat. And when meat was ended, Pwyll said, "Where are the hosts that went yesterday and the day before to the top of the mound?" "Behold, Lord, we are here," said they. "Let us go," said he, "to the mound, to sit there. And do thou," said he to the page who tended his horse, "saddle my horse well, and hasten with him to the road, and bring also my spurs with thee." And the youth did thus. And they went and sat upon the mound; and ere they had been there but a short time, they beheld the lady coming by the same road, and in the same manner, and at the same pace. "Young man," said Pwyll, "I see the lady coming; give me my horse." And no sooner had he mounted his horse than she passed him. And he turned after her and followed her. And he let his horse go bounding playfully, and thought that at the second step or the third he should come up with her. But he came no nearer to her than at first. Then he urged his horse to his utmost speed, yet he found that it availed nothing to follow her.

Then said Pwyll, "O maiden, for the sake of him whom thou best lovest, stay for me." "I will stay gladly," said she, "and it were better for thy horse hadst thou asked it long since." So the maiden stopped, and she threw back that part of her head-dress which covered her face. And she fixed her eyes upon him, and began to talk with him. "Lady," asked he, "whence comest thou, and whereunto dost thou journey?" "I journey on mine own errand," said she, "and right glad am I to see thee." "My greeting be unto thee," said he. Then he thought that the beauty of all the maidens, and all the ladies that he had ever seen, was as nothing compared to her beauty. "Lady," he said, "wilt thou tell me aught concerning thy purpose?" "I will tell thee," said she. "My chief quest was to seek thee." "Behold," said Pwyll, "this is to me the most pleasing quest on which thou couldst have come; and wilt thou tell me who thou art?" "I will tell thee, Lord," said she. "I am Rhiannon, the daughter of Heveydd Hên, and they sought to give me to a husband against my will. But no husband would I have, and that because of my love for thee, neither will I yet have one unless thou reject me. And hither have I come to hear thy answer." "By Heaven," said Pwyll, "behold this is my answer. If I might choose among all the ladies and damsels in the world, thee would I choose." "Verily," said she, "if thou art thus minded, make a pledge to meet me ere I am given to another." "The sooner I may do so, the more pleasing will it be unto me," said Pwyll, "and wheresoever thou wilt, there will I meet with thee." "I will that thou meet me this day twelvemonth at the palace of Heveydd. And I will cause a feast to be prepared, so that it be ready against thou come." "Gladly," said he, "will I keep this tryst." "Lord," said she, "remain in health, and be mindful that thou keep thy promise; and now I will go hence." So they parted, and he went back to his hosts and to them of his household. And whatsoever questions they asked him respecting the damsel, he always turned the discourse upon other matters. And when a year from that time was gone, he caused a hundred knights to equip themselves and to go with him to the palace of Heveydd Hên. And he came to the palace, and there was great joy concerning him, with much concourse of people and great rejoicing, and vast preparations for his coming. And the whole Court was placed under his orders.

And the hall was garnished and they went to meat, and thus did they sit; Heveydd Hên was on one side of Pwyll, and Rhiannon on the other. And all the rest according to their rank. And they ate and feasted and talked one with another, and at the beginning of the carousal after the meat, there entered a tall auburn-haired youth, of royal bearing, clothed in a garment of satin. And when he came into the hall, he saluted Pwyll and his companions. "The greeting of Heaven be unto thee, my soul," said Pwyll, "come thou and sit down." "Nay," said he, "a suitor am I, and I will do mine errand." "Do so willingly," said Pwyll. "Lord," said he, "my errand is unto thee, and it is to crave a boon of thee that I come." "What boon soever thou mayest ask of me, as far as I am able, thou shalt have." "Ah," said Rhiannon, "wherefore didst thou give that answer?" "Has he not given it before the presence of these nobles?" asked the youth. "My soul," said Pwyll, "what is the boon thou askest?" "The lady whom best I love is to be thy bride this night; I come to ask her of thee, with the feast and the banquet that are in this place." And Pwyll was silent because of the answer which he had given. "Be silent as long as thou wilt," said Rhiannon. "Never did man make worse use of his wits than thou hast done." "Lady," said he, "I knew not who he was." "Behold this is the man to whom they would have given me against my will," said she. "And he is Gwawl the son of Clud, a man of great power and wealth, and because of the word thou hast spoken, bestow me upon him lest shame befall thee." "Lady," said he, "I understand not thine answer. Never can I do as thou sayest." "Bestow me upon him," said she, "and I will cause that I shall never be his." "By what means will that be?" asked Pwyll. "In thy hand will I give thee a small bag," said she. "See that thou keep it well, and he will ask of thee the banquet, and the feast, and the preparations which are not in thy power. Unto the hosts and the household will I give the feast. And such will be thy answer respecting this. And as concerns myself, I will engage to become his bride this night twelvemonth. And at the end of the year be thou here," said she, "and bring this bag with thee, and let thy hundred knights be in the orchard up yonder. And when he is in the midst of joy and feasting, come thou in by thyself, clad in ragged garments, and holding thy bag in thy hand, and ask nothing but a bagful of food, and I will cause that if all the meat and liquor that are in these seven Cantrevs were put into it, it would be no fuller than before And after a great deal has been put therein, he will ask thee whether thy bag will ever be full. Say thou then that it never will, until a man of noble birth and of great wealth arise and press the food in the bag with both his feet, saying, 'Enough has been put therein'; and I will cause him to go and tread down the food in the bag, and when he does so, turn thou the bag, so that he shall be up over his head in it, and then slip a knot upon the thongs of the bag. Let there be also a good bugle horn about thy neck, and as soon as thou hast bound him in the bag, wind thy horn, and let it be a signal between thee and thy knights. And when they hear the sound of the horn, let them come down upon the palace." "Lord," said Gwawl, "it is meet that I have an answer to my request." "As much of that thou hast asked as it is in my power to give, thou shalt have," replied Pwyll. "My soul," said Rhiannon unto him, "as for the feast and the banquet that are here, I have bestowed them upon the men of Dyved, and the household, and the warriors that are with us. These can I not suffer to be given to any. In a year from to-night a banquet shall be prepared for thee in this palace, that I may become thy bride."

So Gwawl went forth to his possessions, and Pwyll went also back to Dyved. And they both spent that year until it was the time for the feast at the palace of Heveydd Hên. Then Gwawl the son of Clud set out to the feast that was prepared for him, and he came to the palace, and was received there with rejoicing. Pwyll, also, the Chief of Annwvyn, came to the orchard with his hundred knights, as Rhiannon had commanded him, having the bag with him. And Pwyll was clad in coarse and ragged garments, and wore large clumsy old shoes upon his feet. And when he knew that the carousal after the meat had begun, he went towards the hall, and when he came into the hall, he saluted Gwawl the son of Clud, and his company, both men and women. "Heaven prosper thee," said Gwawl, "and the greeting of Heaven be unto thee." "Lord," said he, "may Heaven reward thee, I have an errand unto thee." "Welcome be thine errand, and if thou ask of me that which is just, thou shalt have it gladly." "It is fitting," answered he. "I crave but from want, and the boon that I ask is to have this small bag that thou seest filled with meat." "A request within reason is this," said he, "and gladly shalt thou have it. Bring him food." A great number of attendants arose and began to fill the bag, but for all that they put into it, it was no fuller than at first. "My soul," said Gwawl, "will thy bag be ever full?" "It will not, I declare to Heaven," said he, "for all that may be put into it, unless one possessed of lands, and domains, and treasure, shall arise and tread down with both his feet the food that is within the bag, and shall say, 'Enough has been put therein.'" Then said Rhiannon unto Gwawl the son of Clud,

"Rise up quickly." "I will willingly arise," said he. So he rose up, and put his two feet into the bag. And Pwyll turned up the sides of the bag, so that Gwawl was over his head in it. And he shut it up quickly and slipped a knot upon the thongs, and blew his horn. And thereupon behold his household came down upon the palace. And they seized all the host that had come with Gwawl, and cast them into his own prison. And Pwyll threw off his rags, and his old shoes, and his tattered array; and as they came in, every one of Pwyll's knights struck a blow upon the bag, and asked, "What is here?" "A Badger," said they. And in this manner they played, each of them striking the bag, either with his foot or with a staff. And thus played they with the bag. Every one as he came in asked, "What game are you playing at thus?" "The game of Badger in the Bag," said they. And then was the game of Badger in the Bag first played.

"Lord," said the man in the bag, "if thou wouldest but hear me, I merit not to be slain in a bag." Said Heveydd Hên, "Lord, he speaks truth. It were fitting that thou listen to him, for he deserves not this." "Verily," said Pwyll, "I will do thy counsel concerning him." "Behold this is my counsel then," said Rhiannon; "thou art now in a position in which it behoves thee to satisfy suitors and minstrels; let him give unto them in thy stead, and take a pledge from him that he will never seek to revenge that which has been done to him. And this will be punishment enough." "I will do this gladly," said the man in the bag. "And gladly will I accept it," said Pwyll, "since it is the counsel of Heveydd and Rhiannon." "Such then is our counsel," answered they. "I accept it," said Pwyll. "Seek thyself sureties." "We will be for him," said Heveydd, "until his men be free to answer for him." And upon this he was let out of the bag, and his liegemen were liberated. "Demand now of Gwawl his sureties," said Heveydd, "we know which should be taken for him." And Heveydd numbered the sureties. Said Gwawl, "Do thou thyself draw up the covenant." "It will suffice me that it be as Rhiannon said," answered Pwyll. So unto that covenant were the sureties pledged. "Verily, Lord," said Gwawl, "I am greatly hurt, and I have many bruises. I have need to be anointed; with thy leave I will go forth. I will leave nobles in my stead, to answer for me in all that thou shalt require." "Willingly," said Pwyll, "mayest thou do thus." So Gwawl went towards his own possessions.

And the hall was set in order for Pwyll and the men of his host, and for them also of the palace, and they went to the tables and sat down. And as they had sat that time twelvemonth, so sat they that night. And they ate, and feasted, and spent the night in mirth and tranquillity. And the time came that they should sleep, and Pwyll and Rhiannon went to their chamber.

And next morning at the break of day, "My Lord," said Rhiannon, "arise and begin to give thy gifts unto the minstrels. Refuse no one to-day that may claim thy bounty." "Thus shall it be gladly," said Pwyll, "both to-day and every day while the feast shall last." So Pwyll arose, and he caused silence to be proclaimed, and desired all the suitors and the minstrels to show and to point out what gifts were to their wish and desire. And this being done, the feast went on, and he denied no one while it lasted. And when the feast was ended, Pwyll said unto Heveydd, "My Lord, with thy permission I will set out for Dyved to-morrow." "Certainly," said Heveydd, "may Heaven prosper thee. Fix also a time when Rhiannon may follow thee." "By Heaven," said Pwyll, "we will go hence together." "Willest thou this, Lord?" said Heveydd. "Yes, by Heaven," answered Pwyll.

And the next day, they set forward towards Dyved, and journeyed to the palace of Narberth, where a feast was made ready for them. And there came to them great numbers of the chief men and the most noble ladies of the land, and of these there was none to whom Rhiannon did not give some rich gift, either a bracelet, or a ring, or a precious stone. And they ruled the land prosperously both that year and the next.

THE ELF MAIDEN

The following tale belongs to the Sámi – the indigenous people of Sápmi, a region that is today encompassed by parts of Russia, Norway, Sweden and Finland. Originally found in J. C. Poestion's nineteenth-century collection *Lappländische Märchen*, this translated version was recorded by twentieth-century folklorist Andrew Lang in *The Brown Fairy Book* – one of a series of fairy-tale collections named after different colours, which bring together stories from around the world. Despite the title, there are no explicit mentions of elves or other fairy folk within the tale itself, yet surely no one who reads it could deny there is something magical about the mysterious maiden whom the stranded young man at the centre of this story marries. As you will see throughout this volume, secrecy is characteristic of fairies, so it is only left to learn if our next protagonist can heed his wife's warnings.

Once upon a time two young men living in a small village fell in love with the same girl. During the winter, it was all night except for an hour or so about noon, when the darkness seemed a little less dark, and then they used to see which of them could tempt her out for a sleigh ride with the Northern Lights flashing above them, or which could persuade her to come to a dance in some neighbouring barn. But when the spring began, and the light grew longer, the hearts of the villagers leapt at the sight of the sun, and a day was fixed for the boats to be brought out, and the great nets to be spread in the bays of some islands that lay a few miles to the north. Everybody went on this expedition, and the two young men and the girl went with them.

They all sailed merrily across the sea chattering like a flock of magpies, or singing their favourite songs. And when they reached the shore, what an unpacking there was! For this was a noted fishing ground, and here they would live, in little wooden huts, till autumn and bad weather came round again.

The maiden and the two young men happened to share the same hut with some friends, and fished daily from the same boat. And as time went on, one of the youths remarked that the girl took less notice of him than she did of his companion. At first he tried to think that he was dreaming, and for a long while he kept his eyes shut very tight to what he did not want to see, but in spite of his efforts, the truth managed to wriggle through, and then the young man gave up trying to deceive himself, and set about finding some way to get the better of his rival.

The plan that he hit upon could not be carried out for some months; but the longer the young man thought of it, the more pleased he was with it, so he made no sign of his feelings, and waited patiently till the moment came. This was the very day that they were all going to leave the islands, and sail back to the mainland for the winter. In the bustle and hurry of departure, the cunning fisherman contrived that their boat should be the last to put off, and when everything was ready, and the sails about to be set, he suddenly called out:

'Oh, dear, what shall I do! I have left my best

knife behind in the hut. Run, like a good fellow, and get it for me, while I raise the anchor and loosen the tiller.'

Not thinking any harm, the youth jumped back on shore and made his way up the steep bank. At the door of the hut he stopped and looked back, then started and gazed in horror. The head of the boat stood out to sea, and he was left alone on the island.

Yes, there was no doubt of it—he was quite alone; and he had nothing to help him except the knife which his comrade had purposely dropped on the ledge of the window. For some minutes he was too stunned by the treachery of his friend to think about anything at all, but after a while he shook himself awake, and determined that he would manage to keep alive somehow, if it were only to revenge himself.

So he put the knife in his pocket and went off to a part of the island which was not so bare as the rest, and had a small grove of trees. From one of these he cut himself a bow, which he strung with a piece of cord that had been left lying about the huts.

When this was ready the young man ran down to the shore and shot one or two sea-birds, which he plucked and cooked for supper.

In this way the months slipped by, and Christmas came round again. The evening before, the youth went down to the rocks and into the copse, collecting all the drift wood the sea had washed up or the gale had blown down, and he piled it up in a great stack outside the door, so that he might not have to fetch any all the next day. As soon as his task was done, he paused and looked out towards the mainland, thinking of Christmas Eve last year, and the merry dance they had had. The night was still and cold, and by the help of the Northern Lights he could almost see across to the opposite coast, when, suddenly, he noticed a boat, which seemed steering straight for the island. At first he could hardly stand for joy, the chance of speaking to another man was so delightful; but as the boat drew near there was something, he could not tell what, that was different from the boats which he had been used to all his life, and when it touched the shore he saw that the people that filled it were beings of another world than ours. Then he hastily stepped behind the wood stack, and waited for what might happen next.

The strange folk one by one jumped on to the rocks, each bearing a load of something that they wanted. Among the women he remarked two young girls, more beautiful and better dressed than any of the rest, carrying between them two great baskets full of provisions. The young man peeped out cautiously to see what all this crowd could be doing inside the tiny hut, but in a moment he drew back again, as the girls returned, and looked about as if they wanted to find out what sort of a place the island was.

Their sharp eyes soon discovered the form of a man crouching behind the bundles of sticks, and at first they felt a little frightened, and started as if they would run away. But the youth remained so still, that they took courage and laughed gaily to each other. 'What a strange creature, let us try what he is made of,' said one, and she stooped down and gave him a pinch.

Now the young man had a pin sticking in the sleeve of his jacket, and the moment the girl's hand touched him she pricked it so sharply that the blood came. The girl screamed so loudly that the people all ran out of their huts to see what was the matter. But directly they caught sight of the man they turned and fled in the other direction, and picking up the goods they had brought with them scampered as fast as they could down to the shore. In an instant, boat, people, and goods had vanished completely.

In their hurry they had, however, forgotten two

things: a bundle of keys which lay on the table, and the girl whom the pin had pricked, and who now stood pale and helpless beside the wood stack.

'You will have to make me your wife,' she said at last, 'for you have drawn my blood, and I belong to you.'

'Why not? I am quite willing,' answered he. 'But how do you suppose we can manage to live till summer comes round again?'

'Do not be anxious about that,' said the girl; 'if you will only marry me all will be well. I am very rich, and all my family are rich also.'

Then the young man gave her his promise to make her his wife, and the girl fulfilled her part of the bargain, and food was plentiful on the island all through the long winter months, though he never knew how it got there. And by-and-by it was spring once more, and time for the fisher-folk to sail from the mainland.

'Where are we to go now?' asked the girl, one day, when the sun seemed brighter and the wind softer than usual.

'I do not care where I go,' answered the young man; 'what do you think?'

The girl replied that she would like to go somewhere right at the other end of the island, and build a house, far away from the huts of the fishing-folk. And he consented, and that very day they set off in search of a sheltered spot on the banks of a stream, so that it would be easy to get water.

In a tiny bay, on the opposite side of the island, they found the very thing, which seemed to have been made on purpose for them; and as they were tired with their long walk, they laid themselves down on a bank of moss among some birches and prepared to have a good night's rest, so as to be fresh for work next day. But before she went to sleep the girl turned to her husband, and said: 'If in your dreams you fancy that you hear strange noises, be sure you do not stir, or get up to see what it is.'

'Oh, it is not likely we shall hear any noises in such a quiet place,' answered he, and fell sound asleep.

Suddenly he was awakened by a great clatter about his ears, as if all the workmen in the world were sawing and hammering and building close to him. He was just going to spring up and go to see what it meant, when he luckily remembered his wife's words and lay still. But the time till morning seemed very long, and with the first ray of sun they both rose, and pushed aside the branches of the birch trees. There, in the very place they had chosen, stood a beautiful house—doors and windows, and everything all complete!

'Now you must fix on a spot for your cow-stalls,' said the girl, when they had breakfasted off wild cherries; 'and take care it is the proper size, neither too large nor too small.' And the husband did as he was bid, though he wondered what use a cow-house could be, as they had no cows to put in it. But as he was a little afraid of his wife, who knew so much more than he, he asked no questions.

This night also he was awakened by the same sounds as before, and in the morning they found, near the stream, the most beautiful cow-house that ever was seen, with stalls and milk-pails and stools all complete, indeed, everything that a cow-house could possibly want, except the cows. Then the girl bade him measure out the ground for a storehouse, and this, she said, might be as large as he pleased; and when the storehouse was ready she proposed that they should set off to pay her parents a visit.

The old people welcomed them heartily, and summoned their neighbours, for many miles round, to a great feast in their honour. In fact, for several weeks there was no work done on the farm at all; and at length the young man and his wife grew tired of so much play, and declared that they must return to their own home. But, before they started on the journey, the wife whispered to her husband: 'Take care to jump over the threshold as quick as you can, or it will be the worse for you.'

The young man listened to her words, and sprang over the threshold like an arrow from a bow; and it was well he did, for, no sooner was he on the other side, than his father-in-law threw a great hammer at him, which would have broken both his legs, if it had only touched them.

When they had gone some distance on the road home, the girl turned to her husband and said: 'Till you step inside the house, be sure you do not look back, whatever you may hear or see.'

And the husband promised, and for a while all was still; and he thought no more about the matter till he noticed at last that the nearer he drew to the house the louder grew the noise of the trampling of feet behind him. As he laid his hand upon the door he thought he was safe, and turned to look. There, sure enough, was a vast herd of cattle, which had been sent after him by his father-in-law when he found that his daughter had been cleverer than he. Half of the herd were already through the fence and cropping the grass on the banks of the stream, but half still remained outside and faded into nothing, even as he watched them.

However, enough cattle were left to make the young man rich, and he and his wife lived happily together, except that every now and then the girl vanished from his sight, and never told him where she had been. For a long time he kept silence about it; but one day, when he had been complaining of her absence, she said to him: 'Dear husband, I am bound to go, even against my will, and there is only one way to stop me. Drive a nail into the threshold, and then I can never pass in or out.'

And so he did.

THE BANSHEE OF THE MAC CARTHYS

Perhaps, at some time or another, you've heard a variation on the saying 'to wail like a banshee'. Maybe you've even wondered what it meant? In that case, this next story is for you. The banshee is a figure of Irish folklore whose scream, simply put, is the precursor to death. Unfortunately, she often gets a bad reputation – what with her association with death and all – but rarely, if ever, is the banshee a danger. She does not kill or mark mortals for death, she is simply a warning – a warning that the end is near. How she knows is another question all together . . . In Thomas Crofton Croker's discussion of various banshee legends in his nineteenth-century collection *Fairy Legends and Traditions of the South of Ireland*, we meet the Mac Carthy family who have their very own banshee – one who marks each family member's inevitable demise.

The family of Mac Carthy have for some generations possessed a small estate in the county of Tipperary. They are the descendants of a race, once numerous and powerful in the south of Ireland; and though it is probable that the property they at present hold is no part of the large possessions of their ancestors, yet the district in which they live is so connected with the name of Mac Carthy by those associations which are never forgotten in Ireland, that they have preserved with all ranks a sort of influence much greater than that which their fortune or connections could otherwise give them. They are, like most of this class, of the Roman Catholic persuasion, to which they adhere with somewhat of the pride of ancestry, blended with a something, call it what you will, whether bigotry, or a sense of wrong, arising out of repeated diminutions of their family possessions, during the more rigorous periods of the penal laws. Being an old family, and especially being an old Catholic family, they have of course their Banshee;

and the circumstances under which the appearance, which I shall relate, of this mysterious harbinger of death took place, were told me by an old lady, a near connection of theirs, who knew many of the parties concerned, and who, though not deficient in understanding or education, cannot to this day be brought to give a decisive opinion as to the truth or authenticity of the story. The plain inference to be drawn from this is, that she believes it, though she does not own it; and as she was a contemporary of the persons concerned—as she heard the account from many persons about the same period, all concurring in the important particulars—as some of her authorities were themselves actors in the scene—and as none of the parties were interested in speaking what was false; I think we have about as good evidence that the whole is undeniably true as we have of many narratives of modern history, which I could name, and which many grave and sober-minded people would deem it very great pyrrhonism to question. This, however, is a point which it is not my province to determine. People who deal out stories of this sort must be content to act like certain young politicians, who tell very freely to their friends what they hear at a great man's table; not guilty of the impertinence of weighing the doctrines, and leaving it to their hearers to understand them in any sense, or in no sense, just as they may please.

Charles Mac Carthy was, in the year 1749, the only surviving son of a very numerous family. His father died when he was little more than twenty, leaving him the Mac Carthy estate, not much encumbered, considering that it was an Irish one. Charles was gay, handsome, unfettered either by poverty, a father, or guardians, and therefore was not, at the age of one-and-twenty, a pattern of regularity and virtue. In plain terms, he was an exceedingly dissipated—I fear I may say debauched young man. His companions were, as may be supposed, of the higher classes of the youth in his neighbourhood, and, in general, of those whose fortunes were larger than his own, whose dispositions to pleasure were therefore under still less restrictions, and in whose example he found at once an incentive and an apology for his irregularities. Besides, Ireland, a place to this day not very remarkable for the coolness and steadiness of its youth, was then one of the cheapest countries in the world in most of those articles which money supplies for the indulgence of the passions: The odious excise-man, with his portentous book in one hand, his unrelenting pen held in the other, or stuck beneath his hat-band, and the ink-bottle ('black emblem of the informer') dangling from his waist-coat-button—went not then from ale-house to ale-house, denouncing all those patriotic dealers in spirit, who preferred selling whiskey, which had nothing to do with English laws (but to elude them), to retailing that poisonous liquor, which derived its name from the British "Parliament," that compelled its circulation among a reluctant people. Or if the gauger—recording angel of the law—wrote down the peccadillo of a publican, he dropped a tear upon the word, and blotted it out for ever! For, welcome to the tables of their hospitable neighbours, the guardians of the excise, where they existed at all, scrupled to abridge those luxuries which they freely shared; and thus the competition in the market between the smuggler, who incurred little hazard, and the personage ycleped fair trader, who enjoyed little protection, made Ireland a land flowing, not merely with milk and honey, but with whiskey and wine. In the enjoyments supplied by these, and in the many kindred pleasures to which frail youth is but too prone, Charles Mac Carthy indulged to such a degree, that just about the time when he had completed his four-and-twentieth year, after a week of great excesses, he was seized with a violent fever, which, from its malignity, and the weakness of his frame, left scarcely a hope of his recovery. His mother, who had at first made many efforts to check his vices, and at last had been obliged to look on at his rapid progress to ruin in silent despair, watched day and night at his pillow. The anguish of parental feeling was blended with that still deeper misery which those only know who have striven hard to rear in virtue and piety a beloved and favourite child; have found him grow up all that their hearts could desire, until he reached manhood; and then, when their pride was highest, and their hopes almost ended in the fulfilment of their fondest expectations, have seen this idol of their affections plunge headlong into a course of reckless profligacy, and, after a rapid career of vice, hang upon the verge of eternity, without the leisure for, or the power of, repentance. Fervently she prayed that, if his life could not be spared, at least the delirium, which continued with increasing violence from the first few hours of his disorder, might vanish before death, and leave enough of light and of calm for making his peace with offended Heaven. After several days, however, nature seemed quite exhausted, and he sunk into a state too like death to be mistaken for the repose of sleep. His face had that pale, glossy, marble look, which is in general so sure a symptom that life has left its tenement of clay. His eyes were closed and sunk; the lids having that compressed and stiffened appearance which seemed to indicate that some friendly hand had done its last office. The lips, half-closed and perfectly ashy, discovered just so much of the teeth as to give to the features of death their most ghastly, but most impressive look. He lay upon his back, with his hands stretched beside him, quite motionless; and his distracted mother, after repeated trials, could discover not the least symptom of animation. The medical man who attended, having tried the usual modes for ascertaining the presence of life, declared at last his opinion that it was flown, and prepared to depart from the house of mourning. His horse was seen to come to the door. A crowd of people who were collected before the windows, or scattered in groups on the lawn in front, gathered round when the door opened. These were tenants, fosterers, and poor relations of the family, with others attracted by affection, or by that interest which partakes of curiosity, but is something more, and which collects the lower ranks round a house where a human being is in his passage to another world. They saw the professional man come out from the hall door and approach his horse; and while slowly, and with a melancholy air, he prepared to mount, they clustered round him with enquiring and wishful looks. Not a word was spoken; but their meaning could not be misunderstood; and the physician, when he had got into his saddle, and while the servant was still holding the bridle, as if to delay him, and was looking anxiously at his face, as if expecting that he would relieve the general suspense, shook his head, and said in a low voice, "It's all over, James;" and moved slowly away. The moment he had spoken, the women present, who were very numerous, uttered a shrill cry, which, having been sustained for about half a minute, fell suddenly into a full, loud, continued and discordant but plaintive wailing, above which occasionally were heard the deep sounds of a man's voice, sometimes in broken sobs, sometimes in more distinct exclamations of sorrow. This was Charles's foster-brother, who moved about in the crowd, now clapping his hands, now rubbing them together in an agony of grief. The poor fellow had been Charles's playmate and companion when a boy, and afterwards his servant; had always been distinguished by his peculiar regard, and loved his young master, as much, at least, as he did his own life.

When Mrs. Mac Carthy became convinced that

the blow was indeed struck, and that her beloved son was sent to his last account, even in the blossoms of his sin, she remained for some time gazing with fixedness upon his cold features; then, as if something had suddenly touched the string of her tenderest affections, tear after tear trickled down her cheeks, pale with anxiety and watching. Still she continued looking at her son, apparently unconscious that she was weeping, without once lifting her handkerchief to her eyes, until reminded of the sad duties which the custom of the country imposed upon her, by the crowd of females belonging to the better class of the peasantry, who now, crying audibly, nearly filled the apartment. She then withdrew, to give directions for the ceremony of waking, and for supplying the numerous visiters of all ranks with the refreshments usual on these melancholy occasions. Though her voice was scarcely heard, and though no one saw her but the servants and one or two old followers of the family, who assisted her in the necessary arrangements, everything was conducted with the greatest regularity; and though she made no effort to check her sorrows, they never once suspended her attention, now more than ever required to preserve order in her household, which, in this season of calamity, but for her would have been all confusion.

The night was pretty far advanced; the boisterous lamentations which had prevailed during part of the day in and about the house had given place to a solemn and mournful stillness; and Mrs. Mac Carthy, whose heart, notwithstanding her long fatigue and watching, was yet too sore for sleep, was kneeling in fervent prayer in a chamber adjoining that of her son:—suddenly her devotions were disturbed by an unusual noise, proceeding from the persons who were watching round the body. First there was a low murmur—then all was silent, as if the movements of those in the chamber were checked by a sudden panic—and then a loud cry of terror burst from all within:—the door of the chamber was thrown open, and all who were not overturned in the press rushed wildly into the passage which led to the stairs, and into which Mrs. Mac Carthy's room opened. Mrs. Mac Carthy made her way through the crowd into her son's chamber, where she found him sitting up in the bed, and looking vacantly around, like one risen from the grave. The glare thrown upon his sunk features and thin lathy frame gave an unearthly horror to his whole aspect. Mrs. Mac Carthy was a woman of some firmness; but she was a woman, and not quite free from the superstitions of her country. She dropped on her knees, and, clasping her hands, began to pray aloud. The form before her moved only its lips, and barely uttered "Mother;"—but though the pale lips moved, as if there was a design to finish the sentence, the tongue refused its office. Mrs. Mac Carthy sprung forward, and catching the arm of her son, exclaimed, "Speak! in the name of God and his saints, speak! are you alive?"

He turned to her slowly, and said, speaking still with apparent difficulty, "Yes, my mother, alive, and——But sit down and collect yourself; I have that to tell, which will astonish you still more than what you have seen." He leaned back upon his pillow, and while his mother remained kneeling by the bedside, holding one of his hands clasped in hers, and gazing on him with the look of one who distrusted all her senses, he proceeded:—"Do not interrupt me until I have done. I wish to speak while the excitement of returning life is upon me, as I know I shall soon need much repose. Of the commencement of my illness I have only a confused recollection; but within the last twelve hours, I have been before the judgment-seat of God. Do not stare incredulously on me—'tis as true as have been my crimes, and, as I trust, shall be my repentance. I saw the awful Judge arrayed in all the terrors which invest him when mercy gives place to justice. The dreadful pomp of offended omnipotence, I saw,—I remember. It is fixed here; printed on my brain in characters indelible; but it passeth human language. What I *can* describe I *will*—I may speak it briefly. It is enough to say, I was weighed in the balance and found wanting. The irrevocable sentence was upon the point of being pronounced; the eye of my Almighty Judge, which had already glanced upon me, half spoke my doom; when I observed the guardian saint, to whom you so often directed my prayers when I was a child, looking at me with an expression of benevolence and compassion. I stretched forth my hands to him, and besought his intercession; I implored that one year, one month might be given to me on earth, to do penance and atonement for my transgressions. He threw himself at the feet of my Judge, and supplicated for mercy. Oh! never—not if I should pass through ten thousand successive states of being—never, for eternity, shall I forget the horrors of that moment, when my fate hung suspended—when an instant was to decide whether torments unutterable were to be my portion for endless ages! But Justice suspended its decree, and Mercy spoke in accents of firmness, but mildness, 'Return to that world in which thou hast lived but to outrage the laws of Him who made that world and thee. Three years are given thee for repentance; when these are ended, thou shalt again stand here, to be saved or lost for ever.'—I heard no more; I saw no more, until I awoke to life, the moment before you entered."

Charles's strength continued just long enough to finish these last words, and on uttering them he closed his eyes, and lay quite exhausted. His mother, though, as was before said, somewhat disposed to give credit to supernatural visitations, yet hesitated whether or not she should believe that, although awakened from a swoon, which might have been the crisis of his disease, he was still under the influence of delirium. Repose, however, was at all events necessary, and she took immediate measures that he should enjoy it undisturbed. After some hours' sleep, he awoke refreshed, and thenceforward gradually but steadily recovered.

Still he persisted in his account of the vision, as he had at first related it; and his persuasion of its reality had an obvious and decided influence on his habits and conduct. He did not altogether abandon the society of his former associates, for his temper was not soured by his reformation; but he never joined in their excesses, and often endeavoured to reclaim them. How his pious exertions succeeded, I have never learnt; but of himself it is recorded, that he was religious without ostentation, and temperate without austerity; giving a practical proof that vice may be exchanged for virtue, without a loss of respectability, popularity, or happiness.

Time rolled on, and long before the three years were ended, the story of his vision was forgotten, or, when spoken of, was usually mentioned as an instance proving the folly of believing in such things. Charles's health, from the temperance and regularity of his habits, became more robust than ever. His friends, indeed, had often occasion to rally him upon a seriousness and abstractedness of demeanour, which grew upon him as he approached the completion of his seven-and-twentieth year, but for the most part his manner exhibited the same animation and cheerfulness for which he had always been remarkable. In company, he evaded every endeavour to draw from him a distinct opinion on the subject of the supposed prediction; but among his own family it was well known that he still firmly believed it. However, when the day had nearly arrived on which the prophecy was, if at all, to be fulfilled, his whole appearance gave such promise of a long and healthy life, that he was persuaded by his friends to ask a large party to an entertainment at Spring House, to celebrate his birth-day. But the occasion of this party, and the circumstances which attended it, will be best learned from a perusal of the following letters, which have been carefully preserved by some relations of his family. The first is from Mrs. Mac Carthy to a lady, a very near connection and valued friend of hers, who lived in the county of Cork, at about fifty miles' distance from Spring House.

"TO MRS BARRY, CASTLE BARRY.

"*Spring House, Tuesday morning,
October 15th, 1752.*

"MY DEAREST MARY,

"I am afraid I am going to put your affection for your old friend and kinswoman to a severe trial. A two days' journey at this season, over bad roads and through a troubled country, it will indeed require friendship such as yours to persuade a sober woman to encounter. But the truth is, I have, or fancy I have, more than usual cause for wishing you near me. You know my son's story. I can't tell you how it is, but as next Sunday approaches, when the prediction of his dream or his vision will be proved false or true, I feel a sickening of the heart, which I cannot suppress, but which your presence, my dear Mary, will soften, as it has done so many of my sorrows. My nephew, James Ryan, is to be married to Jane Osborne (who, you know, is my son's ward), and the bridal entertainment will take place here on Sunday next, though Charles pleaded hard to have it postponed a day or two longer. Would to God—but no more of this till we meet. Do prevail upon yourself to leave your good man for *one* week, if his farming concerns will not admit of his accompanying you; and come to us, with the girls, as soon before Sunday as you can.

"Ever my dear Mary's attached cousin and friend,

"Ann Mac Carthy."

Although this letter reached Castle Barry early on Wednesday, the messenger having travelled on foot, over bog and moor, by paths impassable to horse or carriage, Mrs Barry, who at once determined on going, had so many arrangements to make for the regulation of her domestic affairs (which, in Ireland, among the middle orders of the gentry, fall soon into confusion when the mistress of the family is away), that she and her two younger daughters were unable to leave home until late on the morning of Friday. The eldest daughter remained to keep her father company, and superintend the concerns of the household. As the travellers were to journey in an open one-horse vehicle, called a jaunting car (still used in Ireland), and as the roads, bad at all times, were rendered still worse by the heavy rains, it was their design to make two easy stages; to stop about midway the first night, and reach Spring House early on Saturday evening. This arrangement was now altered, as they found that, from the lateness of their departure, they could proceed, at the utmost, no farther than twenty miles on the first day; and they therefore purposed sleeping at the house of a Mr Bourke, a friend of theirs, who lived at somewhat less than that distance from Castle Barry. They reached Mr Bourke's in safety, after rather a disagreeable drive. What befell them on their journey the next day to Spring House, and after their arrival there, is fully recounted in a letter from the second Miss Barry to her eldest sister.

"*Spring House, Sunday evening,
20th October, 1752.*
"Dear Ellen,
"As my mother's letter, which encloses this, will announce to you briefly the sad intelligence which

I shall here relate more fully, I think it better to go regularly through the recital of the extraordinary events of the last two days.

"The Bourkes kept us up so late on Friday night, that yesterday was pretty far advanced before we could begin our journey, and the day closed when we were nearly fifteen miles distant from this place. The roads were excessively deep, from the heavy rains of the last week, and we proceeded so slowly, that at last my mother resolved on passing the night at the house of Mr Bourke's brother (who lives about a quarter of a mile off the road), and coming here to breakfast in the morning. The day had been windy and showery, and the sky looked fitful, gloomy, and uncertain. The moon was full, and at times shone clear and bright; at others it was wholly concealed behind the thick black and rugged masses of clouds, that rolled rapidly along and were every moment becoming larger, and collecting together as if gathering strength for a coming storm. The wind, which blew in our faces, whistled bleakly along the low hedges of the narrow road, on which we proceeded with difficulty from the number of deep sloughs, and which afforded not the least shelter, no plantation being within some miles of us. My mother, therefore, asked Leary, who drove the jaunting car, how far we were from Mr Bourke's? ''Tis about ten spades from this to the cross, and we have then only to turn to the left into the avenue, ma'am.' 'Very well, Leary: turn up to Mr Bourke's as soon as you reach the cross roads.' My mother had scarcely spoken these words, when a shriek, that made us thrill as if our very hearts were pierced by it, burst from the hedge to the right of our way. If it resembled anything earthly it seemed the cry of a female, struck by a sudden and mortal blow, and giving out her life in one long deep pang of expiring agony. 'Heaven defend us!' exclaimed my mother. 'Go you over the hedge, Leary, and save that woman, if she is not yet dead, while we run back to the hut we just passed, and alarm the village near it.' 'Woman!' said Leary, beating the horse violently, while his voice trembled – 'that's no woman: the sooner we get on, ma'am, the better'; and he continued his efforts to quicken the horse's pace. We saw nothing. The moon was hid. It was quite dark, and we had been for some time expecting a heavy fall of rain. But just as Leary had spoken, and had succeeded in making the horse trot briskly forward, we distinctly heard a loud clapping of hands, followed by a succession of screams, that seemed to denote the last excess of despair and anguish, and to issue from a person running forward inside the hedge, to keep pace with our progress. Still we saw nothing; until, when we were within about ten yards of the place where an avenue branched off to Mr Bourke's to the left, and the road turned to Spring House on the right, the moon started suddenly from behind a cloud and enabled us to see, as plainly as I now see this paper, the figure of a tall thin woman, with uncovered head, and long hair that floated round her shoulders, attired in something which seemed either a loose white cloak or a sheet thrown hastily about her. She stood on the corner hedge, where the road on which we were met that which leads to Spring House, with her face towards us, her left hand pointing to this place, and her right arm waving rapidly and violently, as if to draw us on in that direction. The horse had stopped, apparently frightened at the sudden presence of the figure, which stood in the manner I have described, still uttering the same piercing cries, for about half a minute. It then leaped upon the road, disappeared from our view for one instant, and the next was seen standing upon a high wall a little way up the avenue on which we purposed going, still pointing towards the road to Spring House, but in an attitude of defiance and command, as if prepared to oppose our passage up the avenue. The figure was now quite silent, and its garments, which had before flown loosely in the wind, were closely wrapped around it. 'Go on, Leary, to Spring House, in God's name,' said my mother; 'whatever world it belongs to, we will provoke it no longer.' ''Tis the Banshee, ma'am,' said Leary; 'and I would not, for what my life is worth, go anywhere this blessed night but to Spring House. But I'm afraid there's something bad going forward, or she would not send us there.' So saying, he drove forward; and as we turned on the road to the right, the moon suddenly withdrew its light, and we saw the apparition no more; but we heard plainly a prolonged clapping of hands, gradually dying away, as if it issued from a person rapidly retreating. We proceeded as quickly as the badness of the roads and the fatigue of the poor animal that drew us would allow, and arrived here about eleven o'clock last night. The scene which awaited us you have learned from my mother's letter. To explain it fully, I must recount to you some of the transactions which took place here during the last week.

"You are aware that Jane Osborne was to have been married this day to James Ryan, and that they and their friends have been here for the last week. On Tuesday last, the very day on the morning of which cousin Mac Carthy despatched the letter inviting us here, the whole of the company were walking about the grounds a little before dinner. It seems that an unfortunate creature, who had been seduced by James Ryan, was seen prowling in the neighbourhood in a moody, melancholy state for some days previous. He had separated from her for several months, and, they say, had provided for her rather handsomely; but she had been seduced by the promise of his marrying her; and the shame of her unhappy condition, uniting with disappointment and jealousy, had disordered her intellects. During the whole forenoon of this Tuesday she had been walking in the plantations near Spring House, with her cloak folded tight round her, the hood nearly covering her face; and she had avoided conversing with or even meeting any of the family.

"Charles Mac Carthy, at the time I mentioned, was walking between James Ryan and another, at a little distance from the rest, on a gravel path, skirting a shrubbery. The whole party were thrown into the utmost consternation by the report of a pistol, fired from a thickly planted part of the shrubbery which Charles and his companions had just passed. He fell instantly, and it was found that he had been wounded in the leg. One of the party was a medical man; his assistance was immediately given, and, on examining, he declared that the injury was very slight, that no bone was broken, that it was merely a flesh wound, and that it would certainly be well in a few days. 'We shall know more by Sunday,' said Charles, as he was carried to his chamber. His wound was immediately dressed, and so slight was the inconvenience which it gave, that several of his friends spent a portion of the evening in his apartment.

"On inquiry, it was found that the unlucky shot was fired by the poor girl I just mentioned. It was also manifest that she had aimed, not at Charles, but at the destroyer of her innocence and happiness, who was walking beside him. After a fruitless search for her through the grounds, she walked into the house of her own accord, laughing and dancing and singing wildly, and every moment exclaiming that she had at last killed Mr Ryan. When she heard that it was Charles, and not Mr Ryan, who was shot, she fell into a violent fit, out of which, after working convulsively for some time, she sprung to the door, escaped from the crowd that pursued her, and could never be taken until last night, when she was brought here, perfectly frantic, a little before our arrival.

"Charles's wound was thought of such little consequence, that the preparations went forward, as usual, for the wedding entertainment on

Sunday. But on Friday night he grew restless and feverish, and on Saturday (yesterday) morning felt so ill, that it was deemed necessary to obtain additional medical advice. Two physicians and a surgeon met in consultation about twelve o'clock in the day, and the dreadful intelligence was announced, that unless a change, hardly hoped for, took place before night, death must happen within twenty-four hours after. The wound, it seems, had been too tightly bandaged, and otherwise injudiciously treated. The physicians were right in their anticipations. No favourable symptom appeared, and long before we reached Spring House every ray of hope had vanished. The scene we witnessed on our arrival would have wrung the heart of a demon. We heard briefly at the gate that Mr Charles was upon his death-bed. When we reached the house, the information was confirmed by the servant who opened the door. But just as we entered, we were horrified by the most appalling screams issuing from the staircase. My mother thought she heard the voice of poor Mrs Mac Carthy, and sprung forward. We followed, and on ascending a few steps of the stairs, we found a young woman, in a state of frantic passion, struggling furiously with two men-servants, whose united strength was hardly sufficient to prevent her rushing up-stairs over the body of Mrs Mac Carthy, who was lying in strong hysterics upon the steps. This, I afterwards discovered, was the unhappy girl I before described, who was attempting to gain access to Charles's room, to 'get his forgiveness,' as she said, 'before he went away to accuse her for having killed him.' This wild idea was mingled with another, which seemed to dispute with the former possession of her mind. In one sentence she called on Charles to forgive her, in the next she would denounce James Ryan as the murderer both of Charles and her. At length she was torn away; and the last words I heard her scream were, 'James Ryan, 'twas you killed him, and not I—'twas you killed him, and not I.'

"Mrs Mac Carthy, on recovering, fell into the arms of my mother, whose presence seemed a great relief to her. She wept—the first tears, I was told, that she had shed since the fatal accident. She conducted us to Charles's room, who, she said, had desired to see us the moment of our arrival, as he found his end approaching, and wished to devote the last hours of his existence to uninterrupted prayer and meditation. We found him perfectly calm, resigned, and even cheerful. He spoke of the awful event which was at hand with courage and confidence, and treated it as a doom for which he had been preparing ever since his former remarkable illness, and which he never once doubted was truly foretold to him. He bade us farewell with the air of one who was about to travel a short and easy journey; and we left him with impressions which, notwithstanding all their anguish, will, I trust, never entirely forsake us.

"Poor Mrs Mac Carthy—but I am just called away. There seems a slight stir in the family; perhaps—"

The above letter was never finished. The enclosure to which it more than once alludes told the sequel briefly, and it is all that I have further learned of the family of Mac Carthy. Before the sun had gone down upon Charles's seven-and-twentieth birthday, his soul had gone to render its last account to its Creator.

FORTUNÉE

It is only apt that in a collection of stories featuring fairies we should have another from the 'mother of fairy tales' Marie-Catherine Le Jumel de Barneville, aka Madame d'Aulnoy. Translated by Annie Macdonell, the story of Fortunée is a seventeenth-century French literary fairy tale that follows the orphaned daughter of a poor labourer. Interestingly enough, rather than a fairy godmother, this is one story that features a rare fairy sister. Regardless of the familial relation, however, the fairies of this story are here to help, although even a fairy can't solve every problem. As is typical of such fairy tales, the protagonist must also be willing to help herself, or where would the lesson be? Oh, and in case it's unclear to anyone, as it briefly was to me, *pinks* are a variety of flower . . . you'll understand their significance soon enough.

Once upon a time there was a poor labourer who, knowing he was about to die, wished to leave nothing behind him that his son and daughter could quarrel about after his death, for he loved them tenderly. "Your mother brought me for a dowry," he said, "two stools and a straw mattress. These, with my hen, would have been my only belongings, had not a pot of pinks and a silver ring been given me by a great lady who lived for some time in my poor cottage. When she went away, she said to me: 'My good man, here is a present for you. Be careful to water the pinks, and to keep the ring in a safe place. I may also tell you that your daughter will be wonderfully beautiful. Call her Fortunée; and give her the ring and the pinks to comfort her for being so poor.' So, dear Fortunée," the good man went on, "you shall have both these, and the rest of my belongings I leave to your brother."

The labourer's two children appeared to be satisfied. Their father died, and they wept, and afterwards they shared his belongings without any dispute. Fortunée thought her brother loved her, but once when she was about to sit down on of the stools, he said to her in an angry tone: "You keep your pinks and your ring, but don't meddle with my stool. I like order in my house." Fortunée, who was very gentle, began to cry quietly, and remained standing, while Bedou (that was the brother's name) sat there as fine as if he had been a learned doctor. Supper time came on; Bedou had a beautiful, fresh egg which his only hen had laid, and he threw the shell towards his sister, saying: "See, I have nothing else to give you; if that isn't enough, go and hunt for frogs: there are plenty in the marsh near by". Fortunée answered nothing, but lifting her eyes to heaven she wept again; then she went to her own room. She found it filled with a delicious scent, which she knew, of course, must be from her pinks. She went up to them, saying, in a sad voice: "Pretty pinks, with all your different colours so fair to see, how you comfort my sad heart by your sweet scent. Never fear that I shall let you want for water, or with cruel hand wrench you from your stalks. I shall take care of you, for you are all I have in the world." Then she looked to see if they wanted watering. They were very dry, so she took the pitcher and ran out in the moonlight to the stream some little way off. As she had walked very fast, she sat down on the bank to rest, but hardly had she done so before she saw a lady, whose majestic air beseemed the large number of attendants who accompanied her. Six maids-of-honour held up the train of her robe, while she leaned on two others. Her guards marched before her, richly clad in amaranth velvet embroidered with pearls. They carried an armchair spread with cloth of gold, on which she presently sat down, and a portable canopy was quickly set up over her head. At the same time there were others spreading a table all covered with golden vessels and crystal vases. An excellent supper was served on the banks of the stream, and the soft murmur of the water seemed to blend with the different voices that were singing these words:—

"Soft and low the summer air
Gently stirs the woodlands there;
Bright flowers glittering on the sod
Mark where Flora's feet have trod:
'Neath the cool shades hear the choirs
Of birds that sing their soft desires:
Would you catch the soft notes too?
Lovers plenty wait for you."

Fortunée hid in a little corner, not daring to move, so surprised was she with all that was happening. After a moment the queen said to one of her squires: "It seems to me that I see a shepherdess near that bush. Bring her here." So Fortunée came forward; and though she was naturally very timid, she did not fail to make a deep bow to the queen, and she did it with so much grace that those who saw her were much astonished. Taking the hem of the queen's robe in her hand she kissed it, and then stood before her with her eyes cast down, the pink blush on her cheek showing up the whiteness of her complexion. Altogether you could not fail to see in her manners that air of mild simplicity that is so charming in young people. "What are you doing here?" the queen asked her. "Are you not afraid of robbers?" "Alas! madam," said Fortuntée, "I have only a cotton frock; so what good would it do them to rob a poor shepherdess like me?" "You are not rich then?" replied the queen, smiling. "I am so poor," said Fortunée, "that my whole inheritance from my father is a pot of pinks and a silver ring." "But you have a heart," added the queen. "If some one wished to take it from you, would you give it away?" "I do not know what it means to give away my heart, madam," she replied. "I have always heard that without one's heart one cannot live; that when it is wounded one must die, and in spite of my poverty I am not sorry to live."

"You will always be right, my pretty girl, to defend your heart. But tell me," the queen went on, "did you have a good supper this evening?" "No, madam," said Fortunée, "my brother ate up everything." The queen ordered them to lay a place for her, and setting her down at the table, she gave her all the best things on it. The young shepherdess was so struck with admiration, and so touched with the queen's kindness, that she could hardly eat a morsel. "I would like very much to know," said the queen, "what you were doing so late at the stream." "Madam," she answered, "there is my pitcher; I was fetching water to water my pinks." So saying she bent down to take hold of the pitcher which was near her; but when she showed it to the queen she was much astonished to find it turned into a golden one, all covered with diamonds and filled with deliciously-scented water. She dared not take it away with her, fearing it was not her own. "I give it to you, Fortunée," said the queen. "Go and water the flowers which you take such good care of, and do not forget that the Queen of the Woods means to be a friend to you." At these words the shepherdess threw herself at her feet. "After giving you my very humble thanks, madam," she said, "for the honour you do me, I make so bold as to ask you to wait here a moment. I am going to fetch you the half of what belongs to me, my pot of pinks. It can never be in better hands than yours." "Very well, Fortunée," said the queen, gently stroking her cheeks. "I will remain here till you return." Fortunée took her golden pitcher, and ran to her little room; but while she had been away her brother Bedou had gone in, taken away her pot of pinks, and put a big cabbage in its place. When Fortunée saw this miserable cabbage she was in despair, and hesitated whether she should go back to the stream or not. At last she made up her mind to do so, and kneeling down before the queen she said: "Madam, Bedou has stolen my pot of pinks: I have only my ring left, and I beg you to take it as a proof of my gratitude". "If I take your ring, pretty shepherdess," said the queen, "you will be ruined." "Ah! madam," she answered, with a pretty air of grace, "if I have your favour I cannot be ruined." The queen took Fortunée's ring and put it on her finger. Then she got into her chariot of coral, decked with emeralds, which was drawn by six white horses, more splendid than the equipage of the sun. Fortunée followed her with her eyes as long as she could, till the turns in the forest roads hid her from her sight. Then she went back to Bedou, her mind full of this adventure.

The first thing she did on entering her room

was to throw the cabbage out of the window. But she was much astonished to hear a voice crying: "Ah! you have killed me!" She could not understand what these cries could mean, for cabbages are not in the habit of talking. As soon as it was day, Fortunée, anxious about her pot of pinks, went outside to look for it, and the first thing she found was the miserable cabbage. Giving it a kick, she said: "What are you doing here? Do you think you do as well in my room as my pinks?" "If I had not been put there," replied the cabbage, "I should never have thought of intruding." Fortunée trembled, for she was very much afraid. But the cabbage spoke once more. "If you will only put me back amongst my kind, I will tell you in two words that your pinks are in Bedou's bed." Fortunée, in despair, did not know how to get possession of them, but she was kind enough first to plant the cabbage, and then taking up her brother's favourite hen, she said: "Naughty creature! I shall make you pay for all the trouble that Bedou gives me". "Ah! shepherdess," said the hen, "let me live, and as I am of a very talkative humour, I shall tell you the most interesting things. Do not think that you are the daughter of the labourer in whose house you have grown up. No, fair Fortunée, he was not your father. But the queen who gave you life had already had six daughters, and—as if she could have borne a son if she had wished—her husband and her father-in-law told her they would stab her if she did not give them an heir. The poor queen, in great distress, was about to have another child. They shut her up in a castle, surrounded her with guards, or rather executioners, who were ordered to kill her if she bore another daughter. The princess, terrified at the danger that threatened her, neither ate nor slept. But she had a sister who was a fairy, and she wrote to tell her of her fears. The fairy, too, was to bear a child, whom she knew would be a son. When he was born, therefore, she packed her son comfortably in a basket, which she gave in charge to the winds, telling them to carry the little prince into the queen's room, and exchange him for the daughter whom she would bear. This plan was, however, of no use, for the queen, not receiving news from her sister the fairy, took advantage of the good nature of one of her guards, who pitied her and let her escape by a cord ladder. As soon as you were born, the poor queen, seeking a hiding-place, came to this hut half dead with fatigue and pain. I was an industrious woman," said the hen, "and a good nurse, so she gave you in charge to me, telling me all her sorrows, with which she was so overcome that she died before she had time to tell us what should be done with you. As I have been very fond of talking all my life, I could not keep from telling this adventure. So one day there came here a beautiful lady, to whom I related everything I knew about it. She touched me immediately with her wand, and I was turned into a hen, and never could speak any more. My grief was terrible, and my husband, who was from home when the change occurred, never knew the truth. When he came back he looked for me everywhere, till at last he thought I was drowned, or that the beasts of the forest had devoured me. The same lady who had done me such a wrong passed by here a second time; she ordered him to call you Fortunée, and made him a present of a pot of pinks and a silver ring. But while she was in the hut, there came five-and-twenty of your royal father's guards, who were seeking you with evil intentions. She muttered some words, and they were all turned into green cabbages, one of which it was you threw out of the window last night. I had never heard him speak till now. I myself could not speak either, and I know not how my voice has come back to me."

The princess was very much astonished at the wonders which the hen told her of. She felt stirred with pity for her, and said: "I am deeply sorry, my poor nurse, that you were turned into a hen. I should very much like to give you back your former shape if I could. But despair of nothing. It seems to me that all the things you have just told me about cannot always remain as they are now. Meanwhile I am going to look for my pinks, for I love them better than anything else."

Bedou had gone to the wood, never imagining that Fortunée would think of rummaging in his bed. She was delighted that he was from home, and was hoping she would find no difficulty, when all at once she saw a great quantity of enormous rats ready for fight. They were drawn up in battalions, with the bed in question behind them, and the stools by their sides. Some large mice formed a reserve force, bent on fighting like Amazons. Fortunée was much surprised, and dared not go nearer, for the rats were attacking her, biting her, and making the blood flow. "What!" she cried, "my pinks, my dear pinks, will you remain in such bad company?" All at once the thought struck her that perhaps the perfumed water which she kept in the golden pitcher might have some special virtue, so she ran to fetch it, and threw some drops of it on the host of rats and mice. In a moment the rabble scampered off, each one to his hole, while the princess bore away her beautiful pinks in haste. They were nearly dead, so much in want of water were they, and she poured on them all she had in her golden pitcher. She was smelling them with great delight when she heard a very sweet voice which came from amongst the leaves and which said: "Wonderful Fortunée! behold the happy day so longed for, when I may declare my feelings to you; for the power of your beauty is such, that even flowers are conscious of it". The princess trembling and astonished at having heard a cabbage and a hen talk, and now a pot of pinks, and at having seen an army of rats, turned pale and fainted.

At that moment Bedou arrived. His work and the heat of the sun had so excited him, that when he saw that Fortuntée had come to seek for her pinks, and had found them, he dragged her to the door and put her out. Hardly had her cheeks touched the cool earth before she opened her beautiful eyes, and saw standing by her the Queen of the Woods, ever charming and dignified. "You have a wicked brother," she said to Fortunée, "I saw how cruelly he threw you out here. Do you wish to be revenged on him?" "No, madam," she said, "I do not know what anger is, and his evil nature cannot change mine." "But," said the queen, "I have a strong conviction that this coarse labourer is not your brother; what do you think?" "All the facts that I am aware of go to prove that he is, madam," replied the shepherdess, modestly, "and I must believe them." "What!" said the queen, "have you not heard that you were born a princess?" "I have just heard it," she answered; "yet dare I venture to boast of a thing of which I have no proof?" "Ah, dear child," said the queen, "how I like to see you in this humour! I know now that the obscure bringing up you have had has not stifled the noble blood in your veins. Yes, you are a princess, and it has not been in my power to save you from the misfortunes which you have experienced up till now."

Here she was interrupted by the arrival of a young man, who was fairer than the day. He was dressed in a long doublet of green and gold silk, fastened with large buttons of emeralds and rubies and diamonds. On his head was a crown of pinks, and his hair hung down over his shoulders. As soon as he saw the queen, he bent one knee to the ground and greeted her respectfully. "Ah! dear Pink," she said, "the unhappy term of your enchantment has come to an end by the help of fair Fortunée. What joy to see you!" And she clasped him close in her arms, and then turning towards the shepherdess she said: "Fair princess, I know all that the hen has told you; but what you do not know is, that the zephyrs, whom I had ordered to exchange my son for you, carried him to a flower-bed while they were searching for your mother, who was my sister. Meanwhile a fairy who knew the most secret things, and with whom I had long been on bad terms, so cleverly seized the opportunity she had been on the watch for ever since the birth of my son, that she changed him on the spot into a pot of pinks, and for all my skill I could not prevent this misfortune. Stung with grief, I used all my art to find a remedy, and I could think of nothing better than to bring Prince Pink to the place where you were being brought up, guessing that when you would have watered the flowers with the delicious water which I had in the golden vase, he would speak, he would love you, and that after that nothing would disturb your peace. I had even in my possession the silver ring which it was necessary for me to receive from your hand, as a sign that the hour was at hand when the charm should lose its force, in spite of the rats and the mice that our enemy sent out to hinder you from touching the pinks. So, dear Fortunée, if my son marries you with this ring, your happiness will never end. Look now if the prince seems to you handsome enough to take him for a husband." "Madam," she replied, blushing, "you heap favours on me. I know that you are my aunt, that by your skill the guards sent to kill me were turned into cabbages, and my nurse into a hen. In proposing to marry me to Prince Pink, you do me more honour than I deserve. But, may I tell you why I hesitate? I do not know what his feelings are for me, and I begin to feel for the first time in my life that I would not be satisfied if he did not love me." "Have no doubts on that point, fair princess," said Pink; "for long you have impressed me as you wish to impress me now, and if I had been able to speak, what should I not have told you every day as to how my affection was growing, burning within me? But I am an unfortunate prince to whom you are quite indifferent." Then he repeated these verses to her:—

"Ah! kinder was my lot before,
    When I, a flower, was all your care,

When on my blossoms you set store,
    And happier were that I was fair;

For your dear eyes I bloomed anew;
    For you I gathered perfume sweet;

And when I looked in vain for you
    While far off tarried your feet,

My faded petals told a tale
  Of a poor heart that down would sink,

And a poor life that 'gan to fail.
  Then water cool you'd bid me drink,

And kisses sweet would be my food,
  And I was whole and bloomed again,

My soul aglow with gratitude;
  To prove my passion I was fain;

Oh! how I longed some fairy power
  Would break the charm that bound so fast

My being in a fragile flower:
  My prayers are answered now at last.

I see you, love you, and can speak
  My love, and all my soul's desire—

Only, alas! in vain I seek
  What once was mine. Your looks retire,

Your words their former feeling lack.
  Gods did I of my lot complain?

My human shape I give you back
  Ah, let me be a flower again!"

The princess seemed very pleased with Pink's gallantry, and praised highly the verses he had made on the spot, and though she was not used to hearing verses, she spoke of them like a person of good taste. The queen, who was impatient at seeing her still dressed as a shepherdess, touched her with her wand, and wished for her the richest dresses that ever were seen. At the word her white cotton frock changed into silver brocade embroidered with carbuncles. From her hair, which was piled high on her head, a long veil of gauze and gold fell down. Her black hair sparkled with diamonds, and her complexion, which had been of dazzling whiteness, became like blooming roses, till the prince could hardly bear to look on its brilliancy. "Ah! Fortunée, how beautiful and charming you are!" cried he, with a sigh. "Will you not comfort me in my distress?" "Nay, my son," said the queen, "your cousin will not resist our prayers."

While she was speaking, Bedou passed by on his way to work, and seeing Fortunée like a goddess, he thought he must be dreaming. She called him in a kindly voice, and begged the queen to have pity on him. "What! after having ill-treated you so?" she said. "Ah, madam," replied the princess, "I am incapable of revenge." The queen kissed her, praising her generous feeling. "To please you," she added, "I am going to make the ungrateful Bedou rich." Thereupon his hut became a palace, beautifully furnished and full of money. But his stools did not change, neither did his bed, to remind him of his former state. And the Queen of the Woods sharpened his wits, softened his manners, and changed his face. Then Bedou felt capable of gratitude, and poured out his thanks to the queen and the princess.

Afterwards by a touch of her wand, the cabbages became men, and the hen a woman. Only Prince Pink was dissatisfied, and sighed as he stood by his princess, begging her to look more kindly upon him. At last she consented. She had never seen a handsome prince before, and the handsomest was as nothing to this one. The Queen of the Woods, delighted by so happy a marriage, took every pains to make all the arrangements as sumptuous as possible. The merrymaking went on for several years, and the happiness of this loving couple lasted their whole life long.

THE LEGEND OF THE WOODEN SHOES

The next tale is exemplary of a common folklore trope concerning fairies, where the fair folk lend assistance to deserving humans through domestic work and craftsmanship. In particular it shares a lot in common with the story of 'The Elves and the Shoemaker' that features in the German fairy tale collections of the Brothers Grimm. 'The Legend of the Wooden Shoes', however, hails from the Netherlands and was originally published by William Elliot Griffis in his twentieth-century collection *Dutch Fairy Tales for Young Folks*. It is also a story with a great number of layers – touching on subjects including Dutch history, industrialization, and the relationship between humanity and the natural world, which fairies often represent. In this sense it is also exemplary of how what some consider simple children's stories can actually be incredibly complex and insightful.

In years long gone, too many for the almanac to tell of, or for clocks and watches to measure, millions of good fairies came down from the sun and went into the earth. There, they changed themselves into roots and leaves, and became trees. There were many kinds of these, as they covered the earth, but the pine and birch, ash and oak, were the chief ones that made Holland. The fairies that lived in the trees bore the name of Moss Maidens, or Tree "Trintjes," which is the Dutch pet name for Kate, or Katharine.

The oak was the favorite tree, for people lived then on acorns, which they ate roasted, boiled or mashed, or made into meal, from which something like bread was kneaded and baked. With oak bark, men tanned hides and made leather, and, from its timber, boats and houses. Under its branches, near the trunk, people laid their sick, hoping for help from the gods. Beneath the oak boughs, also, warriors took oaths to be faithful to their lords, women made promises, or wives joined hand in hand around its girth, hoping to have beautiful children. Up among its leafy branches the new babies lay, before they were found in the cradle by the other children. To make a young child grow up to be strong and healthy, mothers drew them through a split sapling or young tree. Even more wonderful, as medicine for the country itself, the oak had power to heal. The new land sometimes suffered from disease called the *val* (or fall). When sick with the *val*, the ground sunk. Then people, houses, churches, barns and cattle all went down, out of sight, and were lost forever, in a flood of water.

But the oak, with its mighty roots, held the soil firm. Stories of dead cities, that had tumbled beneath the waves, and of the famous Forest of Reeds, covering a hundred villages, which disappeared in one night, were known only too well.

Under the birch tree, lovers met to plight their vows, and on its smooth bark was often cut the figure of two hearts joined in one. In summer, the forest furnished shade, and in winter warmth from the fire. In the spring time, the new leaves were a wonder, and in autumn the pigs grew fat on the mast, or the acorns, that had dropped on the ground.

So, for thousands of years, when men made

their home in the forest, and wanted nothing else, the trees were sacred.

But by and by, when cows came into the land and sheep and horses multiplied, more open ground was needed for pasture, grain fields and meadows. Fruit trees, bearing apples and pears, peaches and cherries, were planted, and grass, wheat, rye and barley were grown. Then, instead of the dark woods, men liked to have their gardens and orchards open to the sunlight. Still, the people were very rude, and all they had on their bare feet were rough bits of hard leather, tied on through their toes; though most of them went barefooted.

The forests had to be cut down. Men were so busy with the axe, that in a few years, the Wood Land was gone. Then the new "Holland," with its people and red roofed houses, with its chimneys and windmills, and dykes and storks, took the place of the old Holt Land of many trees.

Now there was a good man, a carpenter and very skilful with his tools, who so loved the oak that he gave himself, and his children after him, the name of Eyck, which is pronounced Ike, and is Dutch for oak. When, before his neighbors and friends, according to the beautiful Dutch custom, he called his youngest born child, to lay the corner-stone of his new house, he bestowed upon her, before them all, the name of Neeltje (or Nellie) Van Eyck.

The carpenter daddy continued to mourn over the loss of the forests. He even shed tears, fearing lest, by and by, there should not one oak tree be left in the country. Moreover, he was frightened at the thought that the new land, made by pushing back the ocean and building dykes, might sink down again and go back to the fishes. In such a case, all the people, the babies and their mothers, men, women, horses and cattle, would be drowned. The Dutch folks were a little too fast, he thought, in winning their acres from the sea.

One day, while sitting on his door-step, brooding sorrowfully, a Moss Maiden and a Tree Elf appeared, skipping along, hand in hand. They came up to him and told him that his ancestral oak had a message for him. Then they laughed and ran away. Van Eyck, which was now the man's full family name, went into the forest and stood under the grand old oak tree, which his fathers loved, and which he would allow none to cut down.

Looking up, the leaves of the tree rustled, and one big branch seemed to sweep near him. Then it whispered in his ear:

"Do not mourn, for your descendants, even many generations hence, shall see greater things than you have witnessed. I and my fellow oak trees shall pass away, but the sunshine shall be spread over the land and make it dry. Then, instead of its falling down, like acorns from the trees, more and better food shall come up from out of the earth. Where green fields now spread, and the cities grow where forests were, we shall come to life again, but in another form. When most needed, we shall furnish you and your children and children's children, with warmth, comfort, fire, light, and wealth. Nor need you fear for the land, that it will fall; for, even while living, we, and all the oak trees that are left, and all the birch, beech, and pine trees shall stand on our heads for you. We shall hold up your houses, lest they fall into the ooze and you shall walk and run over our heads. As truly as when rooted in the soil, will we do this. Believe what we tell you, and be happy. We shall turn ourselves upside down for you."

"I cannot see how all these things can be," said Van Eyck.

"Fear not, my promise will endure."

The leaves of the branch rustled for another moment. Then, all was still, until the Moss Maiden and Trintje, the Tree Elf, again, hand in hand, as they tripped along merrily, appeared to him.

"We shall help you and get our friends, the

elves, to do the same. Now, do you take some oak wood and saw off two pieces, each a foot long. See that they are well dried. Then set them on the kitchen table to-night, when you go to bed." After saying this, and looking at each other and laughing, just as girls do, they disappeared.

Pondering on what all this might mean, Van Eyck went to his wood-shed and sawed off the oak timber. At night, after his wife had cleared off the supper table, he laid the foot-long pieces in their place.

When Van Eyck woke up in the morning, he recalled his dream, and, before he was dressed, hurried to the kitchen. There, on the table, lay a pair of neatly made wooden shoes. Not a sign of tools, or shavings could be seen, but the clean wood and pleasant odor made him glad. When he glanced again at the wooden shoes, he found them perfectly smooth, both inside and out. They had heels at the bottom and were nicely pointed at the toes, and, altogether, were very inviting to the foot. He tried them on, and found that they fitted him exactly. He tried to walk on the kitchen floor, which his wife kept scrubbed and polished, and then sprinkled with clean white sand, with broomstick ripples scored in the layers, but for Van Eyck it was like walking on ice. After slipping and balancing himself, as if on a tight rope, and nearly breaking his nose against the wall, he took off the wooden shoes, and kept them off, while inside the house. However, when he went outdoors, he found his new shoes very light, pleasant to the feet and easy to walk in. It was not so much like trying to skate, as it had been in the kitchen.

At night, in his dreams, he saw two elves come through the window into the kitchen. One, a kabouter, had a box of tools. The other, an elf, seemed to be the guide. The kabouter at once got out his saw, hatchet, auger, long, chisel-like knife, and smoothing plane. At first, the two elves seemed to be quarrelling, as to who should be boss. Then they settled down quietly to work. The kabouter took the wood and shaped it on the outside. Then he hollowed out, from inside of it, a pair of shoes, which the elf smoothed and polished. Then one elf put his little feet in them and tried to dance, but he only slipped on the smooth floor and flattened his nose; but the other fellow pulled the nose straight again, so it was all right. They waltzed together upon the wooden shoes, then took them off, jumped out the window, and ran away.

When Van Eyck put the wooden shoes on, he found that out in the fields, in the mud, and on the soft soil, and in sloppy places, this sort of foot gear was just the thing. They did not sink in the mud and the man's feet were comfortable, even after hours of labor. They did not "draw" his feet, and they kept out the water far better than leather possibly could.

When the Van Eyck vrouw and the children saw how happy Daddy was, they each one wanted a pair. Then they asked him what he called them.

"Klompen," said he, in good Dutch, and klompen, or klomps, they are to this day.

"I'll make a fortune out of this," said Van Eyck. "I'll set up a klomp-winkel (shop for wooden shoes) at once."

So, going out to the blacksmith's shop, in the village, he had the man who pounded iron fashion for him on his anvil, a set of tools, exactly like those used by the kabouter and the elf, which he had seen in his dream. Then he hung out a sign, marked "Wooden blocks for shoes." He made klomps for the little folks just out of the nursery, for boys and girls, for grown men and women, and for all who walked out-of-doors, in the street or on the fields.

Soon klomps came to be the fashion in all the country places. It was good manners, when you went into a house, to take off your wooden shoes and leave them at the door. Even in the towns and cities, ladies wore wooden slippers, especially when walking or working in the garden.

Klomps also set the fashion for soft, warm socks, and stockings made from sheep's wool. Soon, a thousand needles were clicking, to put a soft cushion between one's soles and toes and the wood. Women knitted, even while they walked to market, or gossiped on the streets. The klomp-winkels, or shops of the shoe carpenters, were seen in every village.

When rich beyond his day-dreams, Van Eyck had another joyful night vision. The next day, he wore a smiling countenance. Everybody, who met him on the street, saluted him and asked, in a neighborly way:

"Good-morning, Mynheer Bly-moe-dig (Mr. Cheerful). How do you sail to-day?"

That's the way the Dutch talk—not "how do you do," but, in their watery country, it is this, "How do you sail?" or else, "Hoe gat het u al?" (How goes it with you, already?)

Then Van Eyck told his dream. It was this: The Moss Maiden and Trintje, the wood elf, came to him again at night and danced. They were lively and happy.

"What now?" asked the dreamer, smilingly, of his two visitors.

He had hardly got the question out of his mouth, when in walked a kabouter, all smutty with blacksmith work. In one hand, he grasped his tool box. In the other, he held a curious looking machine. It was a big lump of iron, set in a frame, with ropes to pull it up and let it fall down with a thump.

"What is it?" asked Van Eyck.

"It's a Hey" (a pile driver), said the kabouter, showing him how to use it. "When men say to you, on the street, to-morrow, 'How do you sail?' laugh at them," said the Moss Maiden, herself laughing.

"Yes, and now you can tell the people how to build cities, with mighty churches with lofty towers, and with high houses like those in other lands. Take the trees, trim the branches off, sharpen the tops, turn them upside down and pound them deep in the ground. Did not the ancient oak promise that the trees would be turned upside down for you? Did they not say you could walk on top of them?"

By this time, Van Eyck had asked so many questions, and kept the elves so long, that the Moss Maiden peeped anxiously through the window. Seeing the day breaking, she and Trintje and the kabouter flew away, so as not to be petrified by the sunrise.

"I'll make another fortune out of this, also,"

said the happy man, who, next morning, was saluted as Mynheer Blyd-schap (Mr. Joyful).

At once, Van Eyck set up a factory for making pile drivers. Sending men into the woods, who chose the tall, straight trees, he had their branches cut off. Then he sharpened the trunks at one end, and these were driven, by the pile driver, down, far and deep, into the ground. So a foundation, as good as stone, was made in the soft and spongy soil, and well built houses uprose by the thousands. Even the lofty walls of churches stood firm. The spires were unshaken in the storm.

Old Holland had not fertile soil like France, or vast flocks of sheep, producing wool, like England, or armies of weavers, as in the Belgic lands. Yet, soon there rose large cities, with splendid mansions and town halls. As high towards heaven as the cathedrals and towers in other lands, which had rock for foundation, her brick churches rose in the air. On top of the forest trees, driven deep into the sand and clay, dams and dykes were built, that kept out the ocean. So, instead of the old two thousand square miles, there were, in the realm, in the course of years, twelve thousand, rich in green fields and cattle. Then, for all the boys and girls that travel in this land of quaint customs, Holland was a delight.

THE LADS WHO MET THE TROLLS
IN THE HEDALE WOOD

'The Lads Who Met the Trolls in the Hedale Wood' is a Norwegian folk-tale originally recorded by the nineteenth-century folklorist Peter Christen Asbojørnsen in his collection *Christmas Fireside Stories; or Round the Yule Log* (translated here by Hans Lien Braekstad). As the title gives away, it features a common figure in Nordic mythology and folklore: the troll. Generally on the larger side when it comes to fairies and elves, the Nordic troll has continued to have great literary influence over the years – anyone remember the trolls encountered by Bilbo and co. in J. R. R. Tolkien's *The Hobbit*? Well, not unlike everyone's favourite reluctant adventurer, the two young brothers in this folk-tale are in for a rather dangerous encounter of their own while walking in the woods. Like Bilbo, will they keep their wits about them, though? You'll have to read on to find out.

Once upon a time in the olden days there lived a poor old couple, tenants on a small farm up in Vaage in the Gudbrandsdale. They had many children, and two of the sons, who might be about half grown up, had always to tramp about the parish begging. They knew therefore all the roads and by-roads, and they knew also the short cut to Hedale.

They were one day going there, but as they had heard that some falconers had built themselves a hut at Moela, they thought they would just look in there at the same time and see the birds and how they were caught, so they took the short cut over the Longmoors. But it was so late in the autumn, that the dairymaids had gone away from the dairies on the mountains and they could find neither shelter nor food anywhere. They had therefore to make their way for Hedale, but it was only a slight path, so when the night set in they lost the track, and to make matters worse they could not find the birdcatchers' hut either. Before they knew where they were, they were right in the thick of

Bjolstad wood. They knew they should not be able to get out of the wood that night, so they commenced cutting boughs off the pine trees, made a fire and built a hut of the branches, for they had a hatchet with them. So they gathered heather and moss to make a bed of. Shortly after they had lain down, they heard something which sniffed and snuffed very loudly through the nose. The boys put their ears to the ground and listened attentively to hear whether it were wild beasts or a troll. Just then the sniffing became louder and some one shouted, "I smell Christian blood about here!"

And they heard somebody walking so heavily that the ground shook under their feet. They knew it was the trolls who were about. "Lord help us! what shall we do?" said the youngest lad to his brother.

"Oh, you had better stand under the fir tree, where you are, and be ready to take our bags and make off, when you see them coming; I will look after the hatchet," said the elder brother.

Just then they saw the trolls approaching; they were so big and tall that their heads reached as high as the tops of the fir trees, but they had only one eye amongst the three of them, and this they used in turn. They had a hole in their foreheads, in which they put it and shifted it about with their hands. He who had the eye went first; the others followed behind and kept hold of the first.

"Run away now," said the elder of the lads, "but don't run too far, before you see what happens. Since they have got their eye so high up, they can't see me very well, when I tackle them from behind."

Well, the younger brother ran off and the trolls after him. In the meantime the elder brother got behind them and gave the last troll a cut with the hatchet in the ankle. The troll gave a horrible shriek, which frightened and gave the first troll such a start that the eye fell out of his forehead. But the lad was not slow in picking it up. It was larger than two pint basins put together, and it was so bright, that although the night was pitch dark, he could see as clearly as by daylight, when he looked through it.

When the trolls found that he had taken their eye from them and that he had wounded one of them, they began to threaten him with every kind of evil in existence, if he did not return them the eye at once.

"I am not afraid of trolls or threats either," said the lad, "now I have got three eyes all to myself and you three haven't got any."

"If we don't get our eye back this minute, we'll

turn you into stocks and stones," screeched the trolls.

But the lad thought there was no hurry; he wasn't afraid of witchcraft or their bragging words. If they didn't leave him alone, he would cut away at them all three till they had to crawl along the ground like snakes.

When the trolls heard this they became frightened, and began to use more polite words. They begged him very nicely to give them their eye back again and he should have both silver and gold and everything he wished for. Well, the lad thought that was very fair, but he wanted all the gold and silver first; and so he said, if one of them would go home and fetch as much gold and silver as he and his brother could fill their bags with and give them two good cross-bows of steel in the bargain, they should have their eye again, but until they did this he would keep it.

The trolls screamed and wailed, and said that none of them could go home when they hadn't any eye to see with, but one of them began to bawl out for their old woman, for they also had a gudewife among the three of them. After a while somebody up in the mountains a good way off to the north answered. So the trolls said that she must come with two steel cross-bows and two buckets full of gold and silver, and before very long she was there, I can tell you. When she heard what had happened, she also commenced to threaten them with witchcraft. But the trolls were afraid, and asked her to beware of the little wasp. She had better mind or he might take her eye as well. So she threw down the buckets with the gold and the silver and the cross-bows to them, and made off towards the mountains with the trolls, But since that time no one has heard that the trolls have been walking in the Hedale wood sniffing for Christian blood.

TE KANAWA'S ADVENTURE WITH A TROOP OF FAIRIES

The following story comes from Sir George Grey's nineteenth-century collection *Polynesian Mythology*, originally titled *Ngā mahi ā ngā tūpuna*. The collection itself compiles a large selection of Māori myths and is one of the earliest published works of traditional Māori stories. Grey – originally from Britain – was not Māori himself, however. He compiled these stories first in Māori then translated them into English, based on the oral traditions of different groups in New Zealand he spoke with. The tale of 'Te Kanawa's Adventure with a Troop of Fairies' was, according to Grey's footnotes, told to him by a man named Te Wherowhero, and follows a legendary chief of Waikato – an area located in New Zealand's North Island, Te Ika-a-Māui.

Te Kanawa, a chief of Waikato, was the man who fell in with a troop of fairies upon the top of Puke-more, a high hill in the Waikato district.

This chief happened one day to go out to catch kiwis with his dogs, and when night came on he found himself right at the top of Puke-more. So his party made a fire to give them light, for it was very dark. They had chosen a tree to sleep under—a very large tree, the only one fit for their purpose that they could find; in fact, it was a very convenient sleeping-place, for the tree had immense roots, sticking up high above the ground: they slept between these roots, and made the fire beyond them.

As soon as it was dark they heard loud voices, like the voices of people coming that way; there were the voices of men, of women, and of children, as if a very large party of people were coming along. They looked for a long time, but could see nothing; till at last Te Kanawa knew the noise must proceed from fairies. His people were all dreadfully frightened, and would have run away if they could; but where could they run to? For they were in the midst of a forest, on the top of a lonely mountain, and it was dark night.

For a long time the voices grew louder and more distinct as the fairies drew nearer and nearer, until they came quite close to the fire; Te Kanawa and his party were half dead with fright. At last the fairies approached to look at Te Kanawa, who was a very handsome fellow. To do this, they kept peeping slily over the large roots of the tree under which the hunters were lying, and kept constantly looking at Te Kanawa, whilst his companions were quite insensible from fear. Whenever the fire blazed up brightly, off went the fairies and hid themselves, peeping out from behind stumps and trees; and when it burnt low, back they came close to it, merrily singing as they moved—

"Here you come climbing over Mount Tirangi
To visit the handsome chief of Ngapuhi,
Whom we have done with."*

---

* Te Wherowhero did not remember the whole song, but that this was the concluding verse; it was probably in allusion to their coming to peep at Te Kanawa.

A sudden thought struck Te Kanawa, that he might induce them to go away if he gave them all the jewels he had about him; so he took off a beautiful little figure, carved in green jasper, which he wore as a neck ornament, and a precious carved jasper ear-drop from his ear. Ah, Te Kanawa was only trying to amuse and please them to save his life, but all the time he was nearly frightened to death. However, the fairies did not rush on the men to attack them, but only came quite close to look at them. As soon as Te Kanawa had taken off his neck ornament, and pulled out his jasper ear-ring, and his other ear-ring, made of a tooth of the tiger-shark, he spread them out before the fairies, and offered them to the multitude who were sitting all round about the place; and thinking it better the fairies should not touch him, he took a stick, and fixing it into the ground, hung his neck ornament and ear-rings upon it.

As soon as the fairies had ended their song, they took the shadows of the ear-rings, and handed them about from one to the other, until they had passed through the whole party, which then suddenly disappeared, and nothing more was seen of them.

The fairies carried off with them the shadows of all the jewels of Te Kanawa, but they left behind them his jasper neck ornament and his ear-rings, so that he took them back again, the hearts of the fairies being quite contented at getting the shadows alone; they saw, also, that Te Kanawa was an honest, well-dispositioned fellow. However, the next morning, as soon as it was light, he got down the mountain as fast as he could without stopping to hunt longer for kiwis.

CINDERELLA

If there is one fairy we all might wish to meet it is surely the fairy godmother. And who is a better example of this kindly fairy than she who ensured Cinderella would attend the ball? 'Cinderella' is probably one of the most recognizable and widely told fairy tales throughout history. The earliest version of this story type, in fact, is more than two thousand years old; preserved by the Ancient Greek writer Strabo, it tells the tale of the enslaved woman Rhodopis who eventually marries an Egyptian Pharaoh. Despite their similarities, however, it was not until the seventeenth century, when French author Charles Perrault wrote down his version, that the fairy godmother appeared (as well as the pumpkin). And he was evidently a big fan, for he also added the beloved fairy godmother to the tale of 'Sleeping Beauty'. So, of course, it is Perrault's 'Cinderella' I have included here, translated by Robert Samber.

Once there was a gentleman who married, for his second wife, the proudest and most haughty woman that was ever seen. She had, by a former husband, two daughters of her own humour and they were indeed exactly like her in all things. He had likewise, by another wife, a young daughter, but of unparalleled goodness and sweetness of temper, which she took from her mother, who was the best creature in the world.

No sooner were the ceremonies of the wedding over, but the stepmother began to shew herself in her colours. She could not bear the good qualities of this pretty girl; and the less, because they made her own daughters appear the more odious. She employed her in the meanest work of the house; she scoured the dishes, tables, &c. and rubbed Madam's chamber, and those of Misses, her daughters; she lay up in a sorry garret, upon a wretched straw-bed, while her sisters lay in fine rooms, with floors all inlaid, upon beds of the very newest fashion, and where they had looking-glasses so large, that they might see themselves at their full length, from head to foot.

The poor girl bore all patiently, and dared not tell her father, who would have rattled her off; for his wife governed him intirely. When she had done her work, she used to go into the chimney-corner, and sit down among cinders and ashes, which made her commonly be called Cinder-breech; but the youngest, who was not so rude and uncivil as the eldest, called her Cinderilla. However, Cinderilla, notwithstanding her mean apparel, was a hundred times handsomer than her sisters, tho' they were always dressed very richly.

It happened that the King's son gave a ball, and invited all persons of fashion to it. Our young misses were also invited; for they cut a very grand figure among the quality. They were mightily delighted at this invitation, and wonderfully busy in chusing out such gowns, petticoats, and head-clothes as might best become them. This was a new trouble to Cinderilla; for it was she who ironed her sisters' linen, and plaited their ruffles; they talked all day long of nothing but how they should be dressed. "For my part," said the eldest, "I will wear my red velvet suit, with French trimming." "And I," said the youngest, "shall only have my usual petti-coat; but then, to make amends for that, I will put on my gold-flowered manteau, and my diamond stomacher, which is far from being the most ordinary one in the world." They sent for the best tire-woman they could get, to make up their head-dresses, and adjust their double-pinners, and they had their red brushes, and patches from the fashionable maker.

Cinderilla was likewise called up to them to be consulted in all these matters, for she had excellent notions, and advised them always for the best, nay and offered her service to dress their heads, which they were very willing she should do. As she was doing this, they said to her:

"Cinderilla, would you not be glad to go to the ball?"

"Ah!" said she, "you only jeer at me; it is not for such as I am to go thither."

"Thou art in the right of it," replied they, "it would make the people laugh to see a Cinder-breech at a ball."

Any one but Cinderilla would have dressed their heads awry, but she was very good, and dressed them perfectly well. They were almost two days without eating, so much they were transported with joy; they broke above a dozen of laces in trying to be laced up close, that they might have a fine slender shape, and they were continually at their looking-glass. At last the happy day came; they went to Court, and Cinderilla followed them with her eyes as long as she could, and when she had lost sight of them she fell a-crying.

Her godmother, who saw her all in tears, asked her what was the matter.

"I wish I could——, I wish I could—;" she was not able to speak the rest, being interrupted by her tears and sobbing.

This godmother of hers, who was a Fairy, said to her:

"Thou wishest thou couldest go to the ball, is it not so?"

"Y—es," cried Cinderilla, with a great sigh.

"Well," said her godmother, "be but a good girl, and I will contrive that thou shalt go." Then she took her into her chamber, and said to her:

"Run into the garden, and bring me a pumpkin."

Cinderilla went immediately to gather the finest she could get, and brought it to her godmother, not being able to imagine how this pumpkin could make her go to the ball. Her godmother scooped out all the inside of it, leaving nothing but the rind; which done, she struck it with her wand, and the pumpkin was instantly turned into a fine coach, gilded all over with gold.

She then went to look into her mouse-trap, where she found six mice all alive, and ordered Cinderilla to lift up a little the trap-door, when giving each mouse, as it went out, a little tap with her wand, the mouse was at that moment turned into a fair horse, which altogether made a very fine set of six horses of a beautiful mouse-coloured dapple-grey.

Being at a loss for a coachman, "I will go and see," says Cinderilla, "if there be never a rat in the rat-trap, that we may make a coachman of him."

"Thou art in the right," replied her godmother; "go and look."

Cinderilla brought the trap to her, and in it there were three huge rats. The Fairy made choice of one of the three, which had the largest beard, and, having touched him with her wand, he was turned into a fat jolly coachman, who had the smartest whiskers eyes ever beheld.

After that, she said to her:

"Go again into the garden, and you will find six lizards behind the watering pot; bring them to me."

She had no sooner done so, but her godmother turned them into six footmen, who skipped up immediately behind the coach, with their liveries all bedaubed with gold and silver, and clung as close behind it, as if they had done nothing else their whole lives. The Fairy then said to Cinderilla:

"Well, you see here an equipage fit to go to the ball with; are you not pleased with it?"

"O yes," cried she, "but must I go thither as I am, in these poison nasty rags?"

Her godmother only just touched her with her wand, and, at the same instant, her clothes were turned into cloth of gold and silver, all beset with jewels. This done she gave her a pair of glass-slippers, the prettiest in the whole world.

Being thus decked out, she got up into her coach; but her godmother, above all things, commanded her not to stay till after midnight, telling her, at the same time, that if she stayed at the ball one moment longer, her coach would be a pumpkin again, her horses mice, her coachman a rat, her footmen lizards, and her clothes become just as they were before.

She promised her godmother, she would not fail of leaving the ball before midnight; and then away she drove, scarce able to contain herself for joy. The King's son, who was told that a great Princess, whom no-body knew, was come, ran out to receive her; he gave her his hand as she alighted out of the coach, and led her into the hall, among all the company. There was immediately a profound silence, they left off dancing, and the violins ceased to play, so attentive was every one to contemplate the singular beauty of this unknown new comer. Nothing was then heard but a confused noise of,

"Ha! how handsome she is! Ha! how handsome she is!"

The King himself, old as he was, could not help ogling her, and telling the Queen softly, "that it was a long time since he had seen so beautiful and lovely a creature." All the ladies were busied in considering her clothes and head-dress, that they might have some made next day after the same pattern, provided they could meet with such fine materials, and as able hands to make them.

The King's son conducted her to the most honourable seat, and afterwards took her out to dance with him: she danced so very gracefully, that they all more and more admired her. A fine collation was served up, whereof the young Prince ate not a morsel, so intently was he busied in gazing on her. She went and sat down by her sisters, shewing them a thousand civilities, giving them part of the oranges and citrons which the Prince had presented her with; which very much surprised them, for they did not know her.

While Cinderilla was thus amusing her sisters, she heard the clock strike eleven and three quarters, whereupon she immediately made a curtesy to the company, and hasted away as fast as she could.

Being got home, she ran to seek out her godmother, and after having thanked her, she said, "she could not but heartily wish she might go next day to the ball, because the King's son had desired her." As she was eagerly telling her godmother whatever had passed at the ball, her two sisters knocked at the door which Cinderilla ran to and opened.

"How long you have stayed," cried she, gaping, rubbing her eyes, and stretching herself as if she had been just awaked out of her sleep; she had not, however, any manner of inclination to sleep since they went from home.

"If thou hadst been at the ball," said one of her sisters, "thou wouldst not have been tired with it; there came thither the finest Princess, the most beautiful ever was seen with mortal eyes; she shewed us a thousand civilities, and gave us oranges and citrons." Cinderilla was transported with joy; she asked them the name of that Princess; but they told her they did not know it; and that the King's son was very anxious to learn it, and would give all the world to know who she was. At this Cinderilla, smiling, replied:

"She must then be very beautiful indeed; Lord! how happy have you been; could not I see her? Ah! dear Miss Charlotte, do lend me your yellow suit of cloaths which you wear every day!"

"Ay, to be sure!" cried Miss Charlotte, "lend my cloaths to such a dirty Cinder-breech as thou art; who's the fool then?"

Cinderilla, indeed, expected some such answer, and was very glad of the refusal; for she would have been sadly put to it, if her sister had lent her what she asked for jestingly.

The next day the two sisters were at the ball, and so was Cinderilla, but dressed more magnificently than before. The King's son was always by her, and never ceased his compliments and amorous speeches to her; to whom all this was so far from being tiresome, that she quite forgot what her godmother had recommended to her, so that she, at last, counted the clock striking twelve, when she took it to be no more than eleven; she then rose up, and fled as nimble as a deer.

The Prince followed, but could not overtake her. She left behind one of her glass slippers, which the Prince took up most carefully. She got home, but quite out of breath, without coach or footmen, and in her nasty old cloaths, having nothing left her of all her finery, but one of the little slippers, fellow to that she dropped. The guards at the palace gate were asked if they had not seen a Princess go out; who said, they had seen no-body go out, but a young girl, very meanly dressed, and who had more the air of a poor country wench, than a gentle-woman.

When the two sisters returned from the ball, Cinderilla asked them if they had been well diverted, and if the fine lady had been there. They told her, Yes, but that she hurried away immediately when it struck twelve, and with so much haste, that she dropped one of her little glass slippers, the prettiest in the world, and which the King's son had taken up; that he had done nothing but look at it during all the latter part of the ball, and that most certainly he was very much in love with the beautiful person who owned the little slipper.

What they said was very true; for a few days after, the King's son caused it to be proclaimed by sound of trumpet, that he would marry her whose foot this slipper would just fit. They whom he employed began to try it on upon the Princesses, then the duchesses, and all the Court, but in vain. It was brought to the two sisters, who did all they possibly could to thrust their feet into the slipper, but they could not effect it.

Cinderilla, who saw all this, and knew her slipper, said to them laughing:

"Let me see if it will not fit me?"

Her sisters burst out a-laughing, and began to banter her. The gentleman who was sent to try the slipper, looked earnestly at Cinderilla, and finding her very handsome, said it was but just that she should try, and that he had orders to let every one make tryal. He invited Cinderilla to sit down, and putting the slipper to her foot, he found it went on very easily, and fitted her, as if it had been made of wax. The astonishment her two sisters were in was excessively great, but still abundantly greater, when Cinderilla pulled out of her pocket the other slipper, and put it on her foot. Thereupon, in came her godmother, who having touched, with her wand, Cinderilla's cloaths, made them richer and more magnificent than any of those she had before.

And now her two sisters found her to be that fine beautiful lady whom they had seen at the ball. They threw themselves at her feet, to beg pardon for all the ill treatment they had made her undergo. Cinderilla took them up, and as she embraced them, cried that she forgave them with all her heart, and desired them always to love her.

She was conducted to the young Prince,

dressed as she was; he thought her more charming than ever, and, a few days after, married her.

Cinderilla, who was no less good than beautiful, gave her two sisters lodgings in the palace, and that very same day matched them with two great lords of the court.

THE KILDARE POOKA

The next story comes from the nineteenth-century collection *Legendary Fictions of the Irish Celts* by Patrick Kennedy. Narrated to him by an unnamed girl from Kilcock, a town in County Kildare, Kennedy prefaces the story itself with a brief description of the Irish pooka (or púca) as a fairy similar to the Scottish brownie or the Northern kobold – fairies who are both a help and a hindrance to households and rural communities – similar *if not* for the fact that the pooka was once a 'christened man'. Although this is not the case in all Celtic folk tales, Kennedy's story does introduce a possibility both intriguing and terrifying: can one become a fairy? The why and how of the thing is for you to discover, but this pooka's fate certainly isn't one which should be taken lightly.

Mr. H——R——, when he was alive, used to live a good deal in Dublin, and he was once a great while out of the country on account of the "Ninety-eight" business. But the servants kept on in the big house at Rath——, all the same as if the family was at home. Well, they used to be frightened out of their lives after going to their beds, with the banging of the kitchen door and the clattering of the fire-irons, and the pots, and plates, and dishes. One evening they sat up ever so long, keeping one another in heart with telling stories about ghosts and fetches and that when—what would you have of it?—the little scullery boy that used to be sleeping over the horses, and couldn't get room at the fire, crept into the hot hearth, and when he got tired listening to the stories, sorra fear him but he fell dead asleep.

Well and good, after they were all gone, and the fire raked up, he was woke with the noise of the kitchen door opening, and the trampling of an ass on the kitchen floor. He peeped out, and what should he see but a big grey ass, sure enough, sitting on his currabingo, and yawning before the fire. After a little, he looked about him, and began scratching his ears as if he was quite tired, and says he, "I may as well begin first as last." The poor boy's teeth began to chatter in his head, for says he, "Now he's goin' to ate me;" but the fellow with the long ears and tail on him, had something else to do. He stirred up the fire, and then he brought in a pail of water from the pump, and filled a big pot, that he put on the fire before he went out. He then put in his hand—foot, I mean—into the hot hearth, and pulled out the little boy. He let a roar out of him with the fright, but the pooka only looked at him, and thrust out his lower lip to show how little he valued him, and then he pitched him into his pew again.

Well, he then lay down before the fire till he heard the boil coming on the water, and maybe there wasn't a plate, or a dish, or a spoon on the dresser, that he didn't fetch and put into the pot, and wash and dry the whole bilin' of 'em as well as e'er a kitchenmaid from that to Dublin town. He then put all of them up in their places on the shelves, and, if he didn't give a good sweepin' to the kitchen after all, leave it till again. Then he comes and sits foment the boy, let down one of his ears and cocked up the other, and gave a grin. The poor fellow strove to roar out, but not a dheeg 'ud come out of his throat. The last thing the pooka done was to rake up the fire, and walk out, giving such a slap o' the door that the boy thought the house couldn't help tumbling down.

Well, to be sure, if there wasn't a hullabulloo next morning when the poor fellow told his story! They could talk of nothing else the whole day. One said one thing, another said another, but a fat, lazy scullery girl said the wittiest thing of all. "Musha!" says she, "if the pooka does be cleaning up everything that way when we're asleep, what should we be slaving ourselves for, doing his work?" "*Sha gu dheine*," says another: "them's the wisest words you ever said, Kauth: it's meself won't contradict you."

So said so done. Not a bit of a plate or dish saw a drop of water that evening, and not a besom was laid on the floor, and every one went to bed soon after sundown. Next morning everything was as fine as fire in the kitchen, and the lord mayor might eat his dinner off the flags. It was great ease to the lazy servants, you may depend, and everything went on well till a foolhardy gag of a boy said he would stay up one night and have a chat with the pooka.

He was a little daunted when the door was

thrown open, and the ass marched up to the fire. He didn't open his mouth till the pot was filled, and the pooka lying snug and sausty before the fire.

"Ah then, sir!" says he, at last, picking up courage, "if it isn't taking a liberty, might I ax who you are, and why are you so kind as to do half of the day's work for the girls every night?" "No liberty at all," says the pooka, says he: "I'll tell you, and welcome. I was a servant here in the time of Squire R.'s father, and was the laziest rogue that ever was clothed and fed, and done nothing for it. When my time came for the other world, this is the punishment was laid on me—to come here, and do all this labour every night, and then go out in the cold. It isn't so bad in the fine weather, but if you only knew what it is to stand with your head between your legs, facing the storm, from midnight to sunrise on a bleak winter night!" "And could we do anything for your comfort, my poor fellow?" says the boy. "Musha, I don't know," says the pooka; "but I think a good quilted frieze coat would help to keep the life in me, them long nights." "Why then, in throth, we'd be the ungratefulest of people if we didn't feel for you."

To make a long story short, the next night but two the boy was there again; and if he didn't delight the poor pooka, holding up a fine warm coat before him, it's no matter! Betune the pooka and the man, his legs were got into the four arms of it, and it was buttoned down his breast and his belly, and he was so pleased, he walked up to the glass to see how he looked. "Well," says he, "it's a long lane that has no turning. I am much obliged to yourself and your fellow-servants. Yous have made me happy at last: good-night to you."

So he was walking out, but the other cried, "Och! sure you're going too soon: what about the washing and sweeping?" "Ah, you may tell the girls that they must now get their turn. My punishment was to last till I was thought worthy of a reward for the way I done my duty. You'll see me no more." And no more they did, and right sorry they were for being in such a hurry to reward the ungrateful pooka.

THE SUMS THAT CAME RIGHT

Whilst most of the stories assembled in this collection could be said to take inspiration from the fairies of mythology, folklore, and oral traditions passed down over generations, this final tale is a somewhat more modern take on the fairy as a whole. This is *not* your usual fairy (whatever that may mean), for *this* is the Arithmetic Fairy. Playing on the long-held idea that fairies represent the mysteries of the natural world, here Edith Nesbit reimagines this classic figure of folklore for the twentieth century in her story 'The Sums That Came Right'; what, after all, is more mysterious than maths? And yes, that is the same Edith Nesbit who you may already know as the classic children's author of *The Railway Children* and *Five Children and It*.

"If twenty-seven barrelsful of apples cost £25 13s. 3d., what would the same barrels be worth if they had been packed by a dishonest person, who only put in ⁷/₉ ths of apples in each barrel and the rest sawdust?"

This was the sum.

It does not look very hard, perhaps, to you who have studied ardently for years at a Board School, or a High School, or a Preparatory School for the sons of gentlemen; but to Edwin it looked as hard as a ship's biscuit. But he went for it like a man, and presently produced an Answer and his Master wrote a big curly R across the sum. Perhaps you do not know that a big curly R means Right? As for the answer to the sum, I will try to get a Fellow of Trinity College, Cambridge (who is a very terrible person), to work it out for you, and if he can do it I will put the answer at the end of this story. I cannot work it myself.

Edwin was glad to see the large curly R. He saw it so seldom that to meet it was a real pleasure.

"But what's the use?" he said. "Everything else leads to something else, except lessons. If you put seeds in the garden they come up flowers, unless they're rotten seeds or you forget where you put them. And if you buy a rabbit—well, there it is, unless it dies. And if you eat your dinner—well, you're not hungry any more for an hour or two. But lessons!"

He bit his penholder angrily and put his head into his desk to look for nibs to play Simpkins minor with. You know the game of nibs, of course? He held up the lid of the desk on his head, as I daresay you have often done, and the inside of the desk was darkish, so that the sudden light at the very back of the desk showed quite brightly and unmistakably.

"Those firework fusees, O Crikey!" was Edwin's first thought.

But it was no firework fusee. It was like glow-worms, only a thousand times more bright and white. For it was the light of pure reason, and it glowed from the glorious eyes of the Arithmetic Fairy. You did not know that there was an Arithmetic Fairy? If you knew as much as I do, it would be simply silly for me to try to tell you stories, wouldn't it?

Her wonderful eyes gleamed and flashed straight into the round goggling eyes of the amazed Edwin.

"Upon my word!" she said.

Edwin said nothing.

"Did no one ever tell you?" the fairy went on, shaking out her dress, which was woven of the integral calculus, and trimmed with a dazzling fringe of logarithms. "Did no one ever tell you that the things that happen when you've done your sums right, happen when you're grown up?"

"I don't care what happens then," Edwin dared to say, for the flashing eyes were kind eyes. "I shall be a pirate, or a bushranger, or something."

The fairy drew hersel up, and her graceful garland of simple equations trembled as Edwin breathed heavily.

"A Pirate," said she, "a nice sort of pirate who can't calculate his men's share of the plunder to three-seventeenths of a gold link of the dead captain's chain! A fine bushranger who can't arrange the forty-two bullets from the revolvers of his seven dauntless followers so that each of the fifteen enemies gets his fair share! Go along with you!" said the Arithmetic Fairy.

But Edwin's eyes were, as I said, wide open, goggling.

"I say," he suddenly remarked, "how jolly pretty you are."

The Arithmetic Fairy has but one weakness—a feminine weakness. She loves a pretty speech. If blunt, so much the worse; yet even bluntness . . .

She looked down and played shyly with the bunch of miscellaneous examples in vulgar fractions which adorned her waistband.

"I suppose you can't be expected to understand, yet," she said, and she said it very gently.

Edwin took courage.

"When I do things I want something to happen at once. 'I want a white rabbit and I want it *now*.'"

She did not recognise the quotation.

"Get your Master to set you a little simple multiplication sum in white rabbits," she said. "Goodbye, my child. You'll know me better in time, and as you know me better you'll love me more."

'I . . . you're lovely now," said Edwin.

The Fairy laughed, and spread her dazzling wings glistening with all the glories of the higher mathematics.

Edwin closed dazzled eyes, and opened them as the desk lid shut down on his head, swayed by no uncertain hand. It was the mathematical master's hand, in fact.

A new example was set. And, curiously enough, white rabbits were in it.

"If seven thousand five hundred and sixty-three white rabbits," it began. Edwin, his brain in a whirl, worked it correctly, by a sort of inspiration, like an ancient prophet or a calculating machine.

When he returned, with his books in a strap, to the red villa whose gables meant home for him, he found an excited crowd dancing round the white-painted gates.

The whole of the front garden, as well as most of the back garden, was a seething mass of white rabbits. Seven thousand five hundred and sixty-three there were, to be exact. I alone know this. The joyous Edwin and his distracted parents were never able to count them.

"What a lot of hutches we shall want," Edwin thought gaily. But when his father came home from the Stock Exchange, where he spent his days considering $7^5/_8$ and $10^3/_{32}$—no doubt under the direct guidance of the Arithmetic Fairy—he said at once—

"Send for the poulterer."

This was done. Only one pair of white rabbits remained the property of Edwin, but these, by the power of the Arithmetic Fairy, became ten by Christmas.

The rabbits disposed of, peace spread a longing wing over the villa, but was not allowed to settle.

"Oh, please 'm," the startled cook, cap all crooked, exclaimed in the hall, "the cellar is choke-full of apples—most of 'em bad 'm—*I* never see no one deliver them, nor yet give no receipt."

The cook, for once in a lurid career, spoke truth. The cellar *was* full of apples. Nineteen pounds nineteen and twopence and one-third of a pennyworth—to be accurate.

Edwin went to bed, feeling now quite sure that he had *not* dreamed the Arithmetic Fairy, and anxiously wondering what to-morrow's sums would be about. Not, he trusted, about snakes, or Sunday School teachers.

The next day's sum was about oranges. Edwin did it correctly, and went home a prey to the most golden apprehensions. Nor were these unfounded. The whole of the dining-room and most of the hall—up to the seventh step of the neatly carpeted stairs—was golden with oranges. Edwin's father said some severe things about practical jokers, and sent for the greengrocer. Edwin ate nine $^3/_7$th oranges, and went to bed yellow, but not absolutely unhappy.

But now he was quite sure.

On the following day his sum dealt with elephants, and in such numbers that his father, on returning from business, yielded to a very natural annoyance, and gave notice to his landlord that he should, at Lady Day, leave a villa where elephants and oranges occurred to such an extent.

No one suspected Edwin of having anything to do with these happenings. And indeed, it was not his fault, so how and why could or should he have owned up to it?

I wish I had time to tell you of the events that occurred when Edwin's sums were set in buttered muffins. Of the seventy-five pigs travelling in a circle at varying rates, I can only say that part of this circle ran through Edwin's mother's drawing-room. Nor can I here relate the tale of the three hundred lightning conductors which were suddenly found to be attached to the once happy villa-home. Edwin's mother cried all day when she was not laughing, and people came from far and near to see the haunted house. For when it came to four thousand white owls and a church steeple every one felt that it was more than a mere accident.

Edwin's master had a pretty taste in sums, and about once a term he used to set a sum about canes. Edwin worked that sum wrong on purpose, so I suppose it served him right that the canes should be at home before he was, just as they would have been if he had worked the sum properly, and as he had borrowed his father's razor that morning to sharpen a slate-pencil, the fifty-seven canes were not all thrown away.

But it was the sum about the cistern that convinced Edwin of the desperate need of finding the Arithmetic Fairy, and begging her to take back the present she had made him. It is not polite to ask this, but Edwin had to do it. You see in the sum the cistern had to leak three pints in thirteen minutes and a quarter, but the cistern at home happened to have a little leak of its own already, where Edwin had tried his new drill on it, and the two leaks together managed so well that when Edwin got home he found water dripping from all the top bedroom ceilings and the staircase was a sort of Niagara. It was very exciting—but when the plumber came he let Edwin's father know all about the little drilled hole, and Edwin got the credit of the leak in the sum, which was much larger and most unfair. His father spoke to Edwin about this matter in his study, and it was then that Edwin saw that he must put an end to the sums that came true.

So he went up to his bedroom with his candle

and his arithmetic book. Directly he put the candle on the chest of drawers a big splash of water from the ceiling fell right on the flame and it went out. He had to go right down stairs to get another light. Then he put the candle on the dressing table—splash—out it went. Chair. Splash! Out! At last he got the candle to stay alight on the washhand-stand, which was, by some curious accident, the only dry place in the room.

Then he opened his book. Somewhere in the book he knew there must be something that would fetch the fairy. He said the Multiplication Table up to nine times—after that, as you know, the worst is over. But no fairy appeared.

Then he read aloud the instructions for working the different rules, including the examples given. There was no result.

Then he called to the Fairy—but she did not come.

Then he tried counting. Then counting and calling mixed with other things. Like this:

"Oh, good Fairy! One—two—three—four—five—six—seven; do come and help me! Eight—nine—ten—eleven! Beautiful, dear, kind, lovely fairy! Nine nines are eighty-one! Dear fairy, do come! Seven million two hundred thousand six hundred and fifty-nine! I will always love you if you will come to me now. Three-sevenths of five-ninths of five-twelfths of sixteen-fiftieths. You were so kind the other day. Two and two are four, and three are seven! Do come now—you've no idea what an awful mess you've got me into. Seven nines are sixty-three—though I know you meant it kindly. Dear Fairy. Thirteen from thirty-seven leaves twenty-four. Do come and see what a hole I'm in—do come—and the product will give you the desired result!"

Edwin stopped, out of breath. He looked round him for the Fairy. But his room, with the water dripping from the roof and the wet towels and basins on the floor, was not a fairy-like place. Edwin saw, with a sigh, that it was no go.

"I'll have another go in prep to-morrow," he said. This he did.

The Mathematical Master was pleased with himself that day because he had succeeded in preventing his best boy from yielding to the allurements of the Head-master and the Classical side.

Of course his class knew at once what kind of temper the Mathematical Master was in—you know we always know that—and Edwin ventured to ask that the examples that day might be about a model steam engine.

"Only *one*, sir, please," he was careful to explain.

The Master kindly consented, and by great good fortune the example did not deal with a faulty boiler, nor with any other defect—but concerned itself solely with the model engine's speed. So Edwin knew, when he had worked his sum, exactly what pace the model engine he would find at home would be good for. He worked the sum right.

Then he put his head into his desk and began again.

"Oh, good Fairy, if a sum of £4,700 is to be divided between A, B, and C,—do, do come and help me. Three-tenths of a pound is six shillings, dear Fairy—eleven—twelve—thirteen—fourteen—oh, lovely Fairy—" and so on.

But no Fairy came. And Simpkins minor whispered—

"What are you chunnering about?" and stuck a pin into Edwin's leg. "Can't you do the beastly example?"

Then quite suddenly Edwin knew what he had to do. He made up an example for himself. This was it.

"If 7,535 fairies were in my desk at school and I subtracted 710 and added 1,006, and the rest flew away in 783 equal gangs, how many would be left over in the desk?"

When he had worked it the answer was one.

Very quickly he opened his desk again, and there was the Arithmetic Fairy, looking more lovely than ever in a rich gown of indices, lined with surds, that fell to her feet in osculating curves. In her hand, like a sceptre, shone the starry glory of the binomial theorem. But her eyes were starrier still. She smiled, but her first words were severe.

"You careless boy," she said. "Why can't you learn to be accurate? It's the merest chance you got me. You should have stated your problem more clearly, and you should have said seven thousand *Arithmetic* Fairies. Why suppose you had found one fairy in your desk, and it had been the Grammar Fairy, or the Football Fairy—what would you have done then?"

"*Is* there a Football Fairy?" Edwin asked.

"Of course. There's a fairy for everything you have to learn. There's a Patience Fairy, and a Good-temper Fairy, and a Fairy to teach people to make bread, and another to teach them to make love. Didn't you really know that?"

"No," said Edwin, "but I say, look here—"

"I am looking," she said, fixing her bright eyes on Edwin's goggling ones, exactly as at their first meeting.

"No—I mean—oh—I say—" he said.

"So I hear," she said.

"No, but—no kid," said he.

"Of course there isn't any kid," said she.

"Dear, kind, pretty Fairy," Edwin began again.

"That's better," said the Fairy.

"Didn't you hear all I was saying to you yesterday, when the water was dripping from the ceiling all over the room?"

"From nineteen several spots. Of course I did."

"Well then," said Edwin.

"You mean that you're tired of having things happen when you do your sums correctly? You prefer the old way!"

"Yes, *please*," said Edwin, "if you're sure you don't mind? I know you meant it for kindness, but, oh, it is most beastly, when you get into the thick of it." He was thinking of the elephants, I fancy.

"I only did it to please you," said the Fairy pouting. "I'll make everything as it was before. Does *that* please you? And there's your third wish. You know we always give three wishes. It's customary in the profession. What would you like?"

Edwin had not attended properly to this speech, so he had only heard "as it was before" and then "What would you like?"

So he said, "I should like to see you again some day."

The Arithmetic Fairy smiled at him, and her beauty grew more and more radiant. She had not expected this. "I made sure you would ask for a pony or a cricket bat or a pair of white mice," she said. "You *shall* see me again, Edwin. Goodbye."

And the bright vision faded away in a dim mist of rosy permutations.

When Edwin got home he heard that a model engine had been discovered in the larder, and had been given to his younger brother. There are some wrongs, some sorrows, to which even a pen like mine cannot hope to do justice.

*

Edwin is now a quiet-looking grown-up person in a black frock coat; and his hair is slowly withdrawing itself from the top of his learned head. I suppose it feels itself unworthy to cover so great a brain. The fairy has been with him, unseen, this many a year. The other day he saw her.

He had been Senior Wrangler, of course; that was nothing to Edwin. And he was Astronomer Royal, but that, after all, he had a right to expect.

But it was when he took breath from his researches one day, and suddenly found that he had invented a bran-new Hypernebular Hypothesis—that he thought of the Fairy, and thinking of her, he beheld her. She was lightly poised above a pile of books based on Newton's "Principia," and topped with his own latest work, "The Fourth and Further Dimensions." He knew her at once, and now he appreciated, more than ever in his youth, the radiance of her eyes and of her wings, for now he understood it.

"Dear, beautiful Fairy," he said, "how glad I am to see you again."

"I've been with you all the time," she said. "I wish I could do something more for you. Is there anything you want?"

The great Mathematician who was Edwin ran his hand over his thin hair.

"No," he said, "no." And then he remembered the school and Simpkins minor and the old desk he used to keep firework fusees in. "Unless," he added, "you could make me young again."

She dropped a little tear, clear as a solved problem.

"I can't do *that*," she said. "You can't have *everything*. The only person who could do that for you is the Love Fairy. If you had found her instead of me you would have been always young, but you wouldn't have invented the Hypernebular Hypothesis."

"I suppose I shall never never find her now?" said Edwin, and as he spoke he looked out of the window to the garden, where a girl was gathering roses.

"I wonder!" said she. "The Love Fairy doesn't live in schooldesks or books on Fourth Dimensions."

"I wonder!" said Edwin. "Does the Love Fairy live in gardens?"

"I wonder!" echoed the Arithmetic Fairy, a little sadly, and she spread her bright wings and flew out of the open window and out of this story.

Edwin went out into the rose garden. And did he find the Love Fairy?

I wonder!

*

PS.—The Fellow of Trinity says the answer to that sum is nineteen pounds, nineteen shillings and two pence and one-third of a penny.

Does the Fellow of Trinity speak the truth?

I wonder!

MACMILLAN COLLECTOR'S LIBRARY

**Own the world's great works of literature in
one beautiful collectible library**

Designed and curated to appeal to book lovers everywhere,
Macmillan Collector's Library editions are small enough to
travel with you and striking enough to take pride of place
on your bookshelf. These much-loved literary classics
also make the perfect gift.

Beautifully made, every Macmillan Collector's Library book
adheres to the same high production values. Each hardback
features gilt edges, a ribbon marker and cloth binding, and
every paperback has a bespoke illustrated cover.

Discover a new and exciting anthology or cherish your
favourite classic stories with this elegant collection.

**Macmillan Collector's Library:
own, collect, and treasure**

Discover the full range at
panmacmillan.com/mcl